Thomas Holcroft, John Fenwick

He's much to Blame

A Comedy in five Acts- Fourth Edition

Thomas Holcroft, John Fenwick

He's much to Blame
A Comedy in five Acts· Fourth Edition

ISBN/EAN: 9783744773072

Printed in Europe, USA, Canada, Australia, Japan

Cover: Foto ©Andreas Hilbeck / pixelio.de

More available books at **www.hansebooks.com**

HE'S MUCH TO BLAME,

A COMEDY:

IN FIVE ACTS.

AS PERFORMED AT THE THEATRE ROYAL,
COVENT GARDEN.

FOURTH EDITION.

LONDON:

PRINTED FOR G. G. AND J. ROBINSON,
PATERNOSTER ROW.

———

MDCCXCVIII.

ADVERTISEMENT.

THE author of HE's MUCH TO BLAME is in some small degree indebted to Le Complaifant, a comedy attributed to Monfieur De Ferriol Pont-de-Veyle, and to the tragedy of Clavigo by Goethe.

PROLOGUE.

Prologues, in thefe fagacious days, muft not
Repeat the ftory ; and betray the plot :
For deep laid plots we fometimes have, no doubt ;
'Tis pity you can't always find them out :
The fecret muft be kept ; and not be told :
In this, at leaft, we beat the bards of old :
We can't endure our meaning you fhould guefs,
And here again we boaft complete fuccefs :
Cautious left you the myftery fhould difcover,
We keep you in the dark—till all is over.

Since thefe important points we muft not name,
The title let's difcufs : He's much to blame !
To blame ? Ay, furely ; very much ! But who ?
The author.   Well, that's nothing very new.
And what does blame induce ? Why punifhment.
Rafhly we fin and leifurely repent.

Lured by that tempting bait a nine nights' bonus,
Thefe fcribbling finners multiply upon us !
Then prologues write ; to whine, cajole, and tickle :
Begging you'll burn the rod you've laid in pickle.
Shielding himfelf by thefe and fuch like arts,
He hopes to hurl with furer aim his darts.
But ftrike and cry, when we receive a blow,
Is arrant cowardice ! I told him fo.
He's mad, who would the field of battle tread ;
Unlefs he hoped to have a broken head.
There's honor in fuch fears—he'll win and wear it :
Then give him honor plenty ! Never fpare it.
But, fhould it be your pleafure not to quarrel,
He'll very kindly bear his load of laurel.

DRAMATIS PERSONÆ.

Lord Vibrate,	-	Mr. Quick.
Sir George Verfatile,	-	Mr. Lewis.
Mr. Delaval,	-	Mr. Pope.
Dr. Gofterman,	-	Mr. Murray.
Thompfon,	-	Mr. Davenport.
Williams,	-	Mr. Clarke.
Harry,	-	Mr. Abbot.
Mafter of the Hotel,	-	Mr. Thompfon.
Jenkins,	-	Mr. Rees.
Waiter,	-	Mr. Elurton.
Footman,	-	Mr. Curtis.
Lady Vibrate,	-	Mrs. Mattocks.
Lady Jane,	-	Mifs Betterton.
Maria,	-	Mrs. Pope.
Lucy,	-	Mrs. Gibbs.
Lady Jane's woman,	-	Mrs. Norton.

HE'S MUCH TO BLAME,

A COMEDY.

ACT I.

SCENE I.—*Ringing heard. The hall of a hotel, with a spacious stair-case.*

Enter the MASTER *and* HEAD WAITER *meeting.*

MASTER.

WHY where are all the fellows, Jenkins? Don't you hear the bell No. 9?

JENK. Tom is gone up to anfwer it, fir.

MAS. Who occupies that apartment?

JENK. The handfome youth and girl, that ar-rived late laft night.

MAS. Juft as I was going to bed?

JENK. Yes, fir.

MAS. He is quite a boy.

JENK. Razor has never robbed him of a hair.

MAS. Some ftripling, perhaps, that has run away with his mother's maid.

JENK. They ordered feparate beds.

MAS. Well, fee what they want.

JENK. Yes, fir.

MAS. And, harkye, be attentive the moment you hear Lord and Lady Vibrate, or their daughter, ftirring.

ftirring. People of quality muft never be neglected.

JENK. Oh, no, fir—Here is Dr. Gofterman.

[*Exit.*

SCENE II. *Enter the* DOCTOR.

MAS. Good morrow, Doctor.

DR. Coot morgen, my tear friend. Is de Fiprate family fifible to fee ?

MAS. Not yet.

DR. My lordtfhip und my latyfhip vas fharge
me to be mit dem betime.

MAS. You are a great favourite there, Doctor.

DR. Ya, fair. Dat I am efery vhere.

MAS. You act in a double capacity : phyfician,
and privy counfellor.

DR. Und I am as better in de von as in de
oder.

MAS. Why ay, Doctor, you have a fmooth pleafant manner.

DR. Ya, fair. Dat is my vay. I mix de fyrup
mit all my prefcription.

MAS. Ay, ay, you are a ufeful perfon.

DR. Ya, fair. Dat is my vay. I leave Yar-
many und I com at Englandt mit little money,
und great cunning in de art, und de fcience. I
fhall af de effence, und de cream, und de balfam,
und de fyrup, und de electric, und de magnetic,
und de mineral, und de vegetable, und de air,
und de earfe, und de fea, und all dat vas fubject
under my command. So I make de nation be-
nefit, und myfelf rifh. Dat is my vay.

MAS. Yes; you can tickle the guineas into
your pocket.

DR. Ya, fair. Dat is my vay.

MAS. You have had many patients ?

DR.

Dr. Ya, fair. I af cure toufand und toufand! Dat is my vay.

Mas. And how many have you killed, Doctor?

Dr. Der Teufel, fair! Kill? Ven my patient vas die, dat vas Nature dat vas kill. Ven dey vas cure, dat vas Dr. Von Goftermans. Dat is my vay. No, fair! Dr. Von Goftermans vas kill himfelf, dat oder people may live.

Mas. How do you mean kill yourfelf, Doctor?

Dr. Der Teufel, fair! Vas I not be call here? Vas I not be call dere? Vas I not be call efery vhere? I af hundert und toufand patient dat die efery day, till I vas com. So I vas drive to de city; und dere I vas meet my beften friend, de gout, de apoplexy, und de afthmatica: und den I vas drive to de inn of court, und de lawyer; und dere I vas find more of my beften friend; de hydropica, de rheumatica, und de paralytica.

Mas. What, Doctor! The lawyers and inns of court paralytic?

Dr. Ya, fair.

Mas. I wifh they were, with all my foul!

Dr. Und den I vas drive und make my reverence mit de lordt, und mit de duke, und mit de grandee; und dere I vas meet mofh oder of my beften friend; de hypochondrica, de fpafmodica, de hyfterica, de marafma, de morbid affection, de tremor, und de mift before de eye.

Mas. Morbid affections, tremors, and mifts before the eyes, the difeafes of the great?

Dr. Ya, fair. Und dey vas grow vorfe und vorfe efery day.

Mas. Well, well, they have chofen a fkilful doctor!

Dr. Ya, fair. I fhall do all deir bufinefs, efery von.

von. Dat is my vay. I fhall af de effence, und de cream, und de balfam, und de fyrup, und de electric, und de magnetic, und de mineral, und de vegetable, und de air, und de earfe, und de fea, und all dat vas fubject under my command. Dat is my vay. Bote dat is as noting at all. Ah fa, my liebfte: you vas my beften friend. You make me acquaint myfelf mit all de patient dat vas come to your houfe; and fo I vas your beften friend, und I vas gif de phyfic for yourfelf, und de phyfic for your fhile, und de phyfic for your vife.

MAS. For which my wife will never more thank you, Doctor.

DR. No: your vife vas die, und you vas tank me yourfelf. So now you tell me: Af you any new cuftomer dat vas com?

MAS. Yes: a youth, and a girl that looks like a waiting maid, arrived late laft night.

DR. Vhich it vas a perfon of grandeur?

MAS. Oh no; wholly unattended.

DR. Ah ah! Vhich it vas a lofing couple, den?

MAS. It feems not.

DR. A poy und a vaiting vomans! Dere fhall be fometing myftery in dat.

MAS. So I think. Here comes the girl.

DR. Ah ah! Let me do: I fhall talk to her. I fhall begin by make acquaintance mit her.

SCENE III.   *Enter* LUCY *down the ftaircafe.*

LU. Pray, fir, defire the waiter to make hafte with breakfaft.

MAS. Here, Jenkins! Breakfaft to No. 9! Be quick!

JENK. (*Without*) Yes, fir.

MAS.

Mas. Tea or coffee, madam?

Lu. Tea.

Dr. How you do, my tear? You vas pretty young frau: fery pretty girl, my tear. Perhaps you vas ftranger, my tear?

Lu. Perhaps I am.

Dr. Ah! Vat is your name, my tear?

Lu. That which my Godmother gave me.

Dr. Your maftair af made de long yourney, my tear.

Lu. Has he?

Dr. From vat country you com, my tear?

Lu. Hem!

Dr. I afk, from vat country you com, my tear.

Lu. Afk again.

Dr. From de town of —— Ha!

Lu. Ay. How do you call it?

Dr. Dat is vat I vant you fhall tell?

Lu. I fee you do.

Dr. Your maftair is fery young, my tear.

Lu. Thank you, fir.

Dr. For vat you tank me?

Lu. For your news.

Dr. Ah, ah! You are fery vitty und pretty, my tear.

Lu. More news. Thank you again.

Dr. Vat vas you call de young yentleman's name?

Lu. I will afk, and fend you word.

Dr. How long fhall he be ftay in town?

Lu. Till he goes into the country.

Dr. Vat is your capacity, my tear?

Lu. Like yours, little enough.

Dr. You not underftandt me, my tear. Vat is your poft, your office?

Lu. To anfwer rude queftions.

B

Dr. Your maftair is man of family?

Lu. Yes. He had a father, and mother, and uncles, and aunts.

Dr. Und tey vas tead?

Lu. I am not a tombftone.

Dr. Com, com, my tear, let you make me anfwer.

Lu. Anan?

Enter Waiter.

Wait. Here is the breakfaft, madam.

Lu. Take it up ftairs.

[*Exeunt Lucy and Waiter up the ftaircafe.*

Dr. Der Teufel! A cunning yipfey! She has make me raife my curiofity. *(Calls.)* My tear! My tear! Com pack, my tear! *(Lucy returns.)* Do my compliment to your maftair, und I fhall make me mofh happy if I fhall af de honeur to make me acquaintance mit him. My name is call Dr. Von Gottermans. I fhall af de effence, und de cream, und de balfam, und de fyrup, und de electric, und de magnetic, und de mineral, und de vegetable, und de air, und de earfe, und de fea, und all dat vas fubject under my command. I fhall af de beft recommendation for de honeft Docteur dat vas poffible. My Lordt und my Laty Fiprate vas my beften friend. I vas practice mit all de piggeft family in de uniferfe. Docteur Von Gottermans vas know efery poty; und efery poty vas know Docteur Von Gottermans. You tell him dat, my tear.

Lu. Tell him that? I cannot remember half of it! Are you, fir, acquainted with Lord Vibrate's family?

Dr.

Dr. Ya, my tear. I vas make friendſhip mit dem more as many year.

Lu. And do you know where they are?

Mas. To be ſure he does. They are in this—

Dr. *(Aſide to Maſter.)* Huſh! Silence your tongue! Dere is ſometing myſtery. *(Aloud.)* If you ſhall make me introduce to your maſtair, my tear, I ſhall tell him efery ting und more as dat, my tear. Vill you, my tear?

Lu. I will go and enquire.

Dr. Tank you, my tear. You are fery pretty girl, my tear: fery vitty pretty—Ah! You are ſo ſly cunning little yipſey, my tear. Ah ah! [*Exeunt.*

SCENE IV.

A chamber. Maria *in man's clothes with a letter in her hand and walking with anxiety. The Waiter enters and leaves the breakfaſt. She then reads.*

Mar. " Dear ſiſter, The letter I now write is almoſt needleſs, for I ſhall leave Italy and follow it immediately; having at laſt obtained intelligence of your faithleſs lover. I am ſorry to inform you that, in addition to your unpardonable wrongs, I have my own to vindicate. But I have threatened too long. You have heard of the Earl of Vibrate. He and his family are by this arrived in England; your betrayer accompanies them, and I am in cloſe purſuit.   Paul Delaval."

In what will this end? Muſt they meet? Muſt they fight? Muſt one or both of them fall? Oh horror! Shall I be the cauſe of murder? And whoſe blood is to be ſpilled? That of the moſt generous of brothers, or of the man on whom my firſt and laſt affections have been fixed! Is there no ſafety; no means?

B 2   SCENE

SCENE V. *Enter* LUCY.

Lu. Why look here now, madam, you are letting the breakfaſt grow cold! You have been reading that letter again. I do believe I ſhall never get you to eat any more. Come now, pray do take ſome of this French roll; and I'll pour out the tea. Do! Pray do! Pray do!

MAR. I cannot eat, Lucy: I am eaten. Terror and deſpair are devouring me.

Lu. Dear! Dear! What will all this come to? Did not you promiſe me that, as ſoon as you had got ſafe to London in your diſguiſe, you would be better?

MAR. Can it be? My kind, my gentle, my true hearted George!

Lu. True hearted! No no, madam, he was never true hearted: or he could not ſo ſoon have changed, becauſe his ill fortune changed to good. Every body knows true love never changes.

MAR. What have I done? How have I offended? His careſſes, his proteſtations, his tender endearments! Is then the man in whom my ſoul was wrapt a vil—Oh!

Lu. I declare, madam, if you take on this way, you will break my heart as well as your own. Beſide, you forget all the while what you put on this dreſs and came up to London for.

MAR. Oh no. It was if poſſible to prevent miſchief! Murder!——They have never met. They do not know each other. But how ſhall I diſcover Sir George? Of whom ſhall I enquire?

Lu. If you would but eat your breakfaſt, I do think I could put you in the way.

MAR. You?

Lu.

Lu. Yes.

Mar. By what means?

Lu. Will you eat your breakfaft, then?

Mar. I cannot eat. Speak.

Lu. Why I have juft been talking to an out-
landifh comical Doctor, that fays he is acquainted
with Lord Vibrate.

Mar. Indeed! Where is this Doctor?

Lu. He is waiting without: for I knew you
would wifh to fpeak to him.

Mar. Shew him in immediately.

Lu. I'll tell him you are not well; which is but
too true; though you muft remember, madam,
you are a man. So dry your eyes, forget your mif-
fortunes, and, there, cock your hat, a that fafhion,
and try to fwagger a little; or you will be found
out. You ftand fo like a ftatue, and look fo piti-
ful! Lord, that's not the way! If you are timor-
fome, and filent, and bafhful, nobody on earth
will take you for a youth of fortune and fafhion.

[*Exit.*

Mar. *(In revery.)* If they fhould meet! Heavens! They muft not.

SCENE VI. *Re-enter* Lucy *and* Doctor.

Lu. My mafter is not very well: he eats neither
breakfaft, dinner nor fupper, and gets no fleep.

Dr. He noder eat, noder drink, noder fleep!
Dat is pad! Fery pad! But dat it as noting at all,
my tear. Let me do. You fhall fee prefently py
and py vat is my vay.

Mar. Your fervant, fir.

Dr. Sair, I vas your mofh oblifhc fery omple
fairfant, fair. My name is call Dr. Von Goftermans.

mans. I fhall af de beft recommendation for de honeft Docteur dat vas poffible. I vas practice mit all de piggeft family in de uniferfe. Docteur Von Goftermans is know efery pody; und efery pody is know Dr. Von Goftermans. De pretty coquine yung frau tell me dat you not fery fell. You not eat, you not drink, you not fleep. Dat is pad! Fery pad! Bote dat is as noting at all. You tell me de diagnoftic und de prognoftic of all vat you vill ail; und I fhall make you prefcripe for de anodyne, oder de epipaftic, oder de balfamic, oder de narcotic, oder de diaphoretic, oder de expectoratic, oder de reftoratif, oder de emulfif, oder de incifif; vhich is efery ting fo fhveet und fo delectable as all vat is poffible.

MAR. Your pardon, fir, but I wifh to fee you on bufinefs of another nature.

DR. Ah ah! Someting of de prifate affair! Dat is coot. I fhall be as better for dat as for de oder. I vas know de vorl. I vas know efery pody; und efery pody vas know me. Dat is my vay.

MAR. Perhaps then you happen to know Sir George Verfatile?

DR. Oh, Der Teufel, fair! Ya, ya. Sair Shorge is my beften friend. Vhich it vas fix month dat he vas fucceed to his title und eftate; und den I vas make acquaintance mit him: dat is my vay.

MAR. But he has been abroad fince.

DR. Ya, fair. Ven he vas poor, he vas fall in lofe mit fery pretty yung frau. Bote fo foon as he vas pecome rifh paronet dat vas anoder ting! So
his

his relation und his friend vas sent him to make de Gran tour.

MAR. And he was easily persuaded.

DR. Ya, fair. He vas vat you call fery coot nature: he vas alvay comply.

MAR. Compliance with him is more than a weakness: I fear it is a vice.

DR. So he vas make acquaintance mit Lordt und mit Laty Fiprate: und den he vas tink no more of de pretty yung frau, pecaufe he vas fall in lofe mit anoder.

MAR. Sir! Another! What other?

DR. Vat you shall ail, fair? You shange coleur.

MAR. With whom has he fallen in love?

DR. Mit de taughter of Lordt Fiprate.

MAR. With Lady Jane?

DR. Ya, fair: mit Laty Shane—My cot, fair! vat you shall ail? You not make fall in lofe yourself mit Laty Shane?

MAR. No, no—They are no doubt to be married.

DR. My Cot, fair! you fo pale as deaths—My Cot, you shall faint!

Lu. Faint, indeed! (*Aside*) Bear up, madam. (*Aloud*) My mafter is too much of a man to faint. (*Aside*) I'll run for a glafs of water. [*Exit.*

S C E N E VII.

MAR. The charming Lady Jane—Where is she?

DR. My Lordt und my Laty Fiprate und my Laty Shane vas all in de houfe here.

MAR. In this houfe?

DR. Ya, fair,

MAR. And is Sir George here, too?

DR.

Dr. He is com und go alvay fometime efery tay.

Mar. Are they to be married?

Dr. My Cot, fair! you af de ague fit.

Mar. Are they to be married?

Dr. My Laty Fiprate vas mofh incline to Sair Shorge; und my Lordt vas fometime mofh incline too; und den he vas fometime not mofh incline; und den he vas doubt; und den he vas do me de honeur to confultate mit me.

Mar. And what is your advice?

Dr. My Lordt Fiprate vas my beften friends, und I vas adfice dat he fhall do all as vat he pleafe: und Sair Shorge vas my beften friends too, und I vas adfice dat he fhall do all as vat he pleafe: und my Laty Fiprate vas petter as my beften friends, und den I vas more adfice dat fhe fhall do all as vat fhe pleafe.

Mar. But Lady Jane had another lover?

Dr. Ya, fair. Mr. Delafal vas make lofe mit her. He vas com from de Eaft Indie, und he vas lofe her fery mofh; und fhe vas go mit de family to Italy, und my Laty Fiprate vas make acquaintance mit Sair Shorge, pecaufe he vas fo mofh pleafant und coot humeur, und he fay all as vat fhe fay: vhich vas de vay to alvay make agréable.

Mar. Could you do me the favor to introduce me to Lady Jane?

Dr. Ya, fair. I fhall do all as vat fhall make agréable. Dat is my vay.

SCENE VIII. *Re-enter* Lucy *haftily.*

Lu. (*Afide to her miftrefs*) Oh, madam, don't be terrified, but I declare I have fpilled almoft all the water!

Mar.

MAR. (*Alarmed*) What is the matter?

Lu. He is come!

MAR. Who? Sir George?

Lu. No: don't be frightened: Mr. Delaval, from abroad.

MAR. My brother! Heavens! Did he fee you?

Lu. No. I had a glimpfe of him, and whifked away juft as he ftepped out of the poftchaife.

MAR. Should he meet me in this difguife, what will he fay?

Lu. Send away the Doctor, and let us lock ourfelves up.

MAR. (*To the Doctor*) I muft beg you will excufe me, fir; but it is neceffary at prefent I fhould be alone. With your permiffion, I will fee you again in the afternoon; and, in the mean time— (*Gives money*)

DR. Oh, fair! I vas your mofh oblifhe fery omple fairfant, fair. I fhall make you mofh more fifit; und den you fhall tell me de diagnoftic und de prognoftic ot all vat you vill ail.

Lu. Yes yes, another time.

DR. Und I fhall af de effence, und de cream, und de balfam, und de fyrup, und de electric, und de magnetic, und de mineral, und de vegetable, und de air, und de earfe, und de fea, und all dat vas fubject under my command.

Lu. You have told us all that before.

DR. Und I fhall make you prefcripe for de anodyne, oder de epipaftic, oder de balfamic, oder de foporific, oder de narcotic, oder de diaphoretic, oder de expectoratic, oder de reftoratif, oder de emulfif, oder de incifif, vhich is efery ting fo fhveet und del ctable as all vat is poffible.

C

Lu.

Lu. *(Aſide)* Was ever any thing ſo provoking?
—Pray, ſir, make haſte.

Dr. You ſhall make remembrance of Dr. Von
Goſtermans. I am practice mit all de piggeſt family in de uniferſe. Sair, I vas your moſh obliſhe
fery omple ſairfant, ſair. *(The Doctor goes off talking,
and Lucy locks the door while the ſcene changes.)*

SCENE IX. *The hall of the botel.*

Delaval, Williams, Master *and* Jenkins.

Del. Is the portmanteau ſafe?

Will. Yes, ſir.

Del. And the trunks?

Will. All right.

Del. Have you paid the poſtillions?

Will. Yes, ſir.

Master. *(To Delaval)* This way if you pleaſe,
ſir. Jenkins!

Jenk. Coming, ſir.

Mas. Shew the damaſk room. What will you
pleaſe to have for breakfaſt, ſir?

Del. Nothing.

Mas. Sir!

Del. Any thing.

Mas. Bring tea, coffee, and new laid eggs.

Jenk. In a minute, ſir.

Del. *(To Wiliams)* Obſerve the directions I
gave you. Enquire, immediately, and find if the
Vibrate family be in town?

Will. I will be careful, ſir.—Hay?—*(To Delaval going)*—Sir! Sir!

Del. Well?

Will. Look! Here comes Lord Vibrate's
ſecretary!

SCENE

SCENE X. *Enter* THOMPSON.

DEL. (*To Thompfon*) Mr. Thompfon!

THOM. Ah! Mr. Delaval? I am heartily glad to fee you in England!

DEL. Thank you, my good friend. But how is this? Where is the family? Where is Lady Jane?

THOM. I thought that would be your queftion! They are all in this houfe.

DEL. Indeed!

THOM. I knew, when Lady Jane left Italy, your ftay there would be fhort.

DEL. Ay, ay! The follies and frenzies of the madman are vifible to all eyes, except his own.

THOM. I fee you are diffatisfied.

DEL. Tortured, till my thoughts and temper are fo changed that I am almoft as odious to myfelf as the world is become hateful to me.

THOM. I own, you have fome caufe.

DEL. Would *my* injuries were all! But there are other and ftill deeper ftabs. It is not yet ten months fince I returned from India: my heart how light, my eye how cheerful, and my hand prompt at any commendable act. I could then be moved to joy, and forrow, and every fympathifing paffion. Smiles and mock courtefy paffed current on me, the word of man and woman was taken on truft, and I lived in the funfhine of an open unfufpecting foul. But I am now otherwife taught. I am changed. My better part is brutalized; and the wrongs that lie rankling here have ftripped me of human affections, and made me almoft favage.

THOM. What can be faid? Patience is the—

DEL. Talk not of patience: I muft act. I

C 2

may

may then perhaps enquire whether I have acted rightly ? But I muſt firſt ſee Lady Jane, and Lord Vibrate.

THOM. Shall I inform his lordſhip of your arrival ?

DEL. By no means. Having injured, he may wiſh not to ſee me: and I would not afford him time to invent excuſes, and avoid giving me a hearing. Though my wrongs muſt be endured, they ſhall be told.

THOM. I own, they are great.

DEL. Thoſe that you know are heavy; yet, ſevere as the ſtruggle would be, 'tis poſſible they might be huſhed to reſt: but there are others which blood only can obliterate ! which can only ſleep in death ! Such is the road I muſt travel. Not long ſince nature was jocund, the azure heavens were bright, and pleaſure was in every path ; but now darkneſs, fathomleſs gulphs, guilty terrors, and all the dreadful phantoms of meditated deſolation, lie before me.   [*Exeunt.*

ACT II.

SCENE I.

LORD VIBRATE *at a table with a quarto volume reading.*

LORD VIBRATE.

THE ancient ſceptics doubted of every thing, affirmed nothing, and kept the judgment always in ſuſpenſe: All things, ſaid they, are equally indifferent, uncertain, and indeterminate. The mind is never to aſſent to any thing; that it may never be aſtoniſhed, or diſturbed, but enjoy
                                    a perfect

a perfect calm. *(Rises with important wisdom in his looks)* Such were the maxims of Pyrrho, and his disciples; those renowned sages of antiquity! Well! And such too have been my maxims, practically. All my life have I been wavering, uncertain, and indeterminate! A sagacious sceptic without knowing it; and as it were by instinct! It was but lately I discovered what a wise man I am! And yet it seems to me as if I were scarcely half wise enough, for I am told that I am to doubt of every thing which I find rather difficult. For example: that my wife Lady Vibrate is an extravagant rackety rantipole woman of fashion, can I doubt that? No. That she squanders my money, disturbs my peace, and contradicts for contradiction's sake, can I doubt that? No. Then have I not a daughter to marry, a law suit to begin, and a thousand perplexing affairs so that I do not know which way to turn? Why all this appears true to me: but the sceptics teach that appearances deceive, and that nothing is certain. I may be Lord Vibrate, or I may be the Grand Turk. These doctrines are prodigiously deep. *(Considers)* But I must think of something else just now. I have a thousand things to do, and know as little where to begin as where they will end. Ay! All is uncertainty! *(Rings)* Harry! Edward!

SCENE II. *Enter* JENKINS.

JENK. Did your lordship call?

LORD V. Where are my servants? I want some of my plagues.

JENK. They are ready at hand, my lord. Here is your lordship's secretary.

S C E N E　III.

Enter MR. THOMPSON, *and exit* JENKINS.

LORD V. What is the reason, Mr. Thompson, that nobody waits? Here am I, fretting myself to a mummy for the good of my family, while every body about me is as drowsy as the court of common council after dinner! Have they taken laudanum? Are they in a lethargy? Are they all dead?

THOM. If they were, your lordship would have the goodness to raise them.

LORD V. Don't you know how many people I have to see, and places I have to go to?

THOM. No, my lord.

LORD V. Why, did not I tell you?

THOM. Yes, my lord.

LORD V. Then how can you say you don't know?

THOM. Because I venture to presume, my lord, you do not know yourself.

LORD V. I am distracted with doubts. Harry!

S C E N E　IV.　*Enter Footman.*

HAR. Did your lordship call?

LORD V. Where are you all? What are you about? I think you have lived long enough with me to know my way.

HAR. Yes, my lord: we know it very well.

LORD V. If you are not more attentive, I'll discharge you every one.

HAR. Oh no: *(Half aside)* you will not do that.

LORD V. What are you muttering, sirrah?

HAR. Only, my lord, that we know your way.

LORD V.

Lord V. Order the coach at eleven.

Har. Yes, my lord.

Lord V. No. Order it at one.

Har. Yes, my lord.

Lord V. Come back! Order it in ten minutes, and remember I am not at home. Come back! Don't order it at all.

Har. Muſt viſitors be admitted?

Lord V. Yes. No. I cannot tell. I will conſider. Be within call. Thompſon!

[*Exit Footman.*

Thom. My lord.

Lord V. Step to that picture dealer. I will have the Guido. Yet——'tis a great ſum! No—— It is a maſter piece. I muſt have it. Why don't you go?

Thom. The picture is ſold, my lord.

Lord V. Sold? Gone? Have I loſt it? This is always the way! I am for ever diſappointed. Harry!

Re-enter Footman.

Har. My lord.

Lord V. Did you go with the meſſage to the ſtable keeper, laſt night?

Har. Yes, my lord.

Lord V. Let me know when he comes.

Har. He will come no more, my lord.

Lord V. Come no more?

Har. No, my lord.

Lord V. Why ſo?

Har. He ſays you never know your own mind, my lord.

Lord V. Inſolent fellow!

Har. Dr. Gosterman is below.

Lord V. Admit him. Stay. I cannot see him yet. In half an hour. In ten minutes. By and by.

[*Exit Footman.*

SCENE V.

Lord V. I must not waste my time in these trifles. I must attend to this law business. I wish I could determine. What am I to do, Thompson?

Thom. In what, my lord?

Lord V. The affair of the ejectment. If I once embroil myself in law, there will be no end; and if I do not the consequences are still worse.

Thom. Then they are bad indeed, my lord.

Lord V. 'Tis strange that I can come to no resolution, on this subject.

Thom. (*Aside.*) Nor on any other.

Lord V. I must decide this very day, or the time will be elapsed.

Thom. A lawyer I should suppose, my lord, would give you the best advice.

Lord V. How? Are you mad, Thompson? A lawyer give good advice!

Thom. The present possessor has held the estate twenty years.

Lord V. Not till tomorrow. I have time still to make my claim. How shall I act?——Shall I never leave this hotel?——Has the builder been here?

Thom. No, my lord.

Lord V. I can get nothing done. My whole life long I have been distracted with the multiplicity of my affairs.

Thom. And so I am afraid, my lord, you always will be.

Lord

Lord V. Why so, sir?

Thom. Because your lordship undertakes so much, and does so little.

Lord V. So he has not been here?

Thom. No, my lord.

Lord V. Nor the lawyers?

Thom. No, my lord.

Lord V. Nor my steward?

Thom. No, my lord.

Lord V. Nor Sir George?

Thom. No, my lord.

Lord V. Where is Lady Vibrate? Where is Lady Jane? Are they all in their graves? Have none of them shewn signs of life yet?

Thom. Not one. Your lordship is the only person in the family who begin your miseries so soon in a morning.

Lord V. The crosses and cares that prey upon me are enough to make any man on earth miserable.

Thom. Pardon me, my lord, but if you would care less both yourself and your servants would sleep the more. My lady cares for nothing; and she can sleep, when she is in bed, and sing and dance and laugh at your lordship's cares and fears, when she is up.

Lord V. She will drive me mad!

Thom. (*Going.*) Ah! Here she is, as it were for the purpose.

Lord V. Tell Harry to admit the Doctor—No. Not just yet. Yes. In five minutes. I don't know when. [*Exit Thompson.*

D SCENE

SCENE VI. *Enter* LADY VIBRATE.

LADY V. Upon my honor, my lord, you are the most insupportable person imaginable. You vociferate worse than the man who calls when my carriage stops the way. Is any body dying? Is the house on fire? Is the world at an end?

LORD V. By the life your ladyship leads, I should suppose it is pretty near.

LADY V: You always give me such shocking head-achs of a morning.

LORD V. You always give me such shocking heart-achs of an evening.

LADY V. Did not I send to you last night, to request your lordship would not disturb me?

LORD V. It has been your ladyship's amusement to disturb me all your life.

LADY V. Your lordship knows I love amusement.

LORD V. I have not slept a wink since.

LADY V. You had slept quite enough before. Pray how long are we to remain in this hotel? Your lordship should remember, it is degrading for a man of rank to doze away life, in the stile of a colonel reduced to half pay.

LORD V. Your ladyship should remember, it is degrading for a woman of rank to riot away life, and reduce her creditors to live without pay.

LADY V. Pshaw! That is the old story.

LORD V. But it is a very true story. It is a great misfortune that persons so opposite should pair.

LADY V. A terrible one indeed. I am all gaiety and good humour: you are all turmoil and lamentation. I sing, laugh, and welcome pleasure

wherever

wherever I find it: you take your lantern to look for misery, which the sun itself cannot discover.

Lord V. I am overwhelmed by crosses and vexations; and you participate in none of them.

Lady V. No. Heaven be praised!

Lord V. Will you attend to me, my lady, for half an hour?

Lady V. Mercy! Attend to you for half an hour! You, my lord, may think proper to be as miserable as Job: but I am not Job's wife.

Lord V. I insist, Lady Vibrate, on a serious answer. How ought I to act? What should I do, in this law affair?

Lady V. I cannot tell what you ought to do: but I know what you will do.

Lord V. Do you? What?

Lady V. Nothing.

Lord V. The recovery of this property would enable me to give my daughter a portion suitable to her rank. If it is lost, she will be almost destitute of fortune.

Lady V. You should have thought of that before, my lord.

Lord V. Before? Why I have thought of nothing else for years. I have asked every body's advice.

Lady V. And followed nobody's.

Lord V. It shall be so. The ejectment shall be served: proceedings shall commence.

Lady V. Ha, ha, ha!

Lord V. I say, they shall. I am determined.

Lady V. Ha, ha, ha! I know you, my lord.

Lord V. You know! I say they shall, if it be only to prove that you know nothing of the matter.

Lady

LADY V. Ha, ha, ha! A pleafant motive! But even that will not be ftrong enough.

LORD V. But it will, my lady.

LADY V. But it won't, my lord.

SCENE VII. *Enter* DR. GOSTERMAN.

LORD V. I fay it will, my lady.

LADY V. I fay it won't, my lord.

DR. Coot morgen, to my coot lordt und my coot laty.

LORD V. For heaven's fake, Doctor, ftop my lady's tongue.

LADY V. For heaven's fake, Doctor, give my lord a quieting draught.

DR. I fhall do efery ting as vat you defire, my coot lordt und my coot laty.

LORD V. Can nothing filence you, Lady Vibrate? Shall I never have a quiet hearing? I want to talk with you and the Doctor on a thoufand things.

LADY V. Yes; you wifh to have all the talk to yourfelf.

LORD V. On the marriage of our daughter.

LADY V. Oh, with all my heart. A marriage at leaft begins with mufic, feafting, and dancing. So fay on.

LORD V. I am not yet determined in favor of Sir George.

LADY V. But I am. (*While they fpeak, the Doctor gefticulates in favor of each.*)

LORD V. Mr Delaval is an unobjectionable gentleman; and he was the firft fuitor.

LADY V. Sir George can fing; Sir George can dance; Sir George has air, grace, fafhion, and fortune.

LORD V.

LORD V. Pſhaw! His beſt qualities are prudence, and attention to his own concerns. Aſk the Doctor.

DR. He has fery moſh prudence, my coot lordt.

LADY V. Ha, ha ha! I vow, Sir George is the moſt airy, thoughtleſs, pleaſant perſon living: except myſelf.

DR. Ya; Sair Shorge is fery moſh pleaſant: und my latyſhip is fery moſh more pleaſant.

LORD V. Abſurd. His humour is calm, cold, and ſerious.

DR. Fery ſerious, inteet.

LADY V. Whimſical, animated, delightful.

DR. Fery animate, fery telightful, upon my vordt.

LORD V. I never met a more diſcreet ſenſible man in my life.

LADY V. True: for he thinks of nothing but his pleaſures.

LORD V His affairs, you mean.

LADY V. I tell you, my lord, he is exactly what I wiſh: the very ſoul of levity, whim, and laughter.

LORD V. I tell you, my lady, he is exactly like myſelf: prudent, and full of ſage heſitation. He conſiders before he acts. Does he not, Doctor?

DR. Dat vas all yuſt as vat you ſay, my coot lordt.

LADY V. He never conſiders at all. Does he, Doctor?

DR. Dat vas all yuſt as vat you ſay, my coot laty.

LORD V. How ſo? We cannot both be right.

DR. You ſhall pleaſe to make me parton, my coot lordt. Sair Shorge vas all as vat you ſay;
und

und all as vat my coot laty fay.   Mit my laty, he vas merry: mit my lordt, he vas fad.   Mit my laty, he vas laugh, und vas fing, und vas tance: und he vas make melancholy, und mifery, und vas do all dat fhall make agréable mit my lordt.

LORD V. Is he fo variable?

DR. Ya, he vas fery mofh comply: fery mofh coot humeur.   He vas alvay make agréable. Bote vas my lordtfhip und my latyfhip know dat Mr. Delafal vas com from Italy?

LADY V. Come where? To England?

DR. He vas in de houfe below.   I vas fee und fpeak mit his falet.

LORD V. In this hotel?

DR. He vas yuft arrife, und vas demandt dat he fhall fee my lordtfhip; oder my latyfhip.

LADY V. I am very forry he is here.   He is a dun of the moft difagreeable kind, and fhall not fee me; and I hope, my lord, you will no longer permit his addreffes to Lady Jane.   My word is given to Sir George.   Come with me, Doctor.
[*Exeunt Lady Vibrate and Doctor.*

S C E N E VIII.   *Enter* MR. DELAVAL.

DEL. Pardon me, my lord, if I intrude with too little ceremony.   Something I hope will be allowed to a mind much difturbed, and a heart deeply wounded and impatient to eafe its pangs.

LORD V. Which way deeply wounded, Mr. Delaval?

DEL. Can your lordfhip afk? Was it not with your permiffion I paid my addreffes to Lady Jane? And was the ardour of my affection or the extent of my hopes unknown?

LORD

Lord V. Why, I did permit, and I did not. I had my doubts.

Del. My vifits were daily, their purpofe was declared, and I fhould imagine I fpoke more refpectfully to fay that you permitted than that you connived at them.

Lord V. True : but ftill I had my doubts.

Del. Thofe doubts have ftung me to the foul ; and I could wifh you had expreffed them more decidedly.

Lord V. Impoffible! Doubts here, doubts there, doubts every where. No rational man can be decided, on any point whatever. My doubts are my continual plagues : my whole life is confumed by them,

Del. It appears, my lord, you have conquered them on one fubject.

Lord V. Ay indeed ! I wifh to heaven I had ! What fubject is that?

Del. You have affianced your daughter to Sir George Verfatile.

Lord V. Humph!—Yes ; and no. I have ; and I have not. I cannot determine. Sir George is a prudent man, his eftate is large, and the Verfatiles are an ancient race. But your family is ancient, you are prudent, and the wealth left by your uncle is at leaft equal. What can I fay? What can I do ? I don't know which to take nor which to refufe. I am everlaftingly in thefe difficulties. I am haraffed night and day by them : they are the night mare, they fit upon my bofom, opprefs me, fuffocate me. I cannot act. I cannot move.

Del. This, my lord, may be an apology to yourfelf, but the confequence to me is mifery. Your daughter lived in my heart : with her I had pro-

mifed

mifed myfelf ages of happinefs; and had cherifhed
a paffion, impatient perhaps, but, ardent and pure
as her own thoughts. This paffion your conduct
authorized. My fortune, my life, my foul, were
devoted to her. Mine was no light or wanton
dalliance; nor did I expect a light and wanton
conduct from the noble family of which your
lordfhip is the head.

LORD V. What do you mean, Mr. Delaval? I
told you I was undecided; and fo I am ftill. My
lady, you know, was never much your friend. Sir
George is her favourite.

DEL. And is Lady Jane equally changeable?

LORD V. I don't know. She is *my* daughter;
and, judging by myfelf, I fhould fuppofe fhe is
perplexed, and doubtful. She never, I believe,
declared in your favour?

DEL. Not exprefsly, my lord. She referred
me to time and you. 'Tis true I flattered myfelf
her affections were wholly mine. Should fhe prefer Sir George, or any other man, be my feelings
what they will, I then am filenced. My heart
could not be fatisfied with cold compliance. Oh
no! 'Tis of a different ftamp. I am told fhe is
not at home. I hope however fhe will not have
the cruelty to deny me a laft interview: till when
I take my leave. Only fuffer me to remark that,
had you difcovered in me any fecret vice, any de-
fects dangerous to the happinefs of the woman I
adore, you then were juftified in your prefent conduct. But, if you have no fuch accufation to prefer, I muft do my feelings the violence to declare
I cannot but think it highly unworthy of a man of
honor.   [*Exit.*

SCENE

SCENE IX.

LORD V. Mr. Delaval—Infolent!—Highly unworthy of a man of honor ?—I will challenge him.
—He fhall find whether I am a man of honor, or
no. I will challenge him. Harry !

SCENE X. *Enter Footman.*

HAR. My lord.

LORD V. Run. Tell that Mr. Delaval—Hold
—Yes, fly! Tell him—Stay. Get me pen ink and
paper—I will teach him to infult—No. I will not
do him the honor to write. Order him back.

HAR. Order who, my lord ?

LORD V. He fhall give me fatisfaction. In that
at leaft I am determined. He fhall give—And
yet what is fatisfaction ? Is it to be run through
the body? Shot through the head ? A man may
then indeed be faid to be fatisfied—I had forgotten
my doubts on duelling—Tell my lady I wifh to
fpeak to her. No—

HAR. She is here, my lord. [*Exit.*

SCENE XI. *Enter* LADY VIBRATE *and the* DOCTOR.

LADY V. What is the matter, my lord ? You
feem to be even in a worfe humour than ufual !

LORD V. Mr. Delaval has treated me difrefpect-
fully !

LADY V. Have not I a thoufand times told you
he is a difagreeable impertinent perfon ?

LORD V. Why, God forgive me, but I really
find myfelf of your ladyfhip's opinion ! 'Tis a
thing I believe that never happened before !

LADY V. And a thing I believe that will never

E   happen

happen again! I hope, my lord, you are now determined in favor of Sir George?

LORD V. Pofitively. Finally. I pledge my honor.

LADY V. You hear, Doctor.

DR. Ya, my coot laty; I vas hear.

LORD V. I fay, I pledge my honor. I authorife you, my lady, to deliver that meffage to the baronet: and, that I may not have time to begin to doubt, I will inftantly be gone.   [*Exit.*

S C E N E XII.

LADY V. This is fortunate!

DR. Oh, fery mofh fortunate! fery mofh!

LADY V. Had Mr. Delaval married my daughter, we fhould have had a continual fermon on reafon, common fenfe, and good order! And thefe and fuch like antediluvian notions muft have been introduced to our family.

DR. Ah, dat fhall be pad! fery pad inteet, my coot laty!

LADY V. Now that Sir George is the man, the danger is over.

DR. Dat is creat pleffing!

LADY V. But what think you are my daughter's thoughts? I fear fhe has a kind of efteem for Delaval. He was her firft lover.

DR. Ya; fhe vas fery mofh efteem Mr. Delaval, my coot laty.

LADY V. But I obferve fhe liftens with great pleafure to the gay prattle of Sir George.

DR. Oh! fery creat inteet, my coot laty.

LADY V. We muft fecond the rifing paffion: for we muft get rid of that folemn fir.

DR. Dat vas all yuft as vat you fay, my coot laty.

LADY

LADY V. Go to her, Doctor; convince her how intolerable it will be to have a hufband whom fhe cannot quarrel with, nor reproach. Paint in the moft lively colours the ftupid life fhe muft lead, with fo reafonable a man.

DR. I fhall do efery ting as vat fhall make agréable, my coot laty. Dat is my vay. My laty, I vas your mofh oblifhe fery omple fairfant, my laty.   *[Exeunt.*

END OF ACT II.

ACT III.

SCENE I. *The hall of the hotel.* WILLIAMS *and* HARRY. LUCY *fpeaking to the mafter of the hotel.*

WILL.

ALL you fay is very true, Mr. Harry. Our mafters fuppofe we have neither fenfe nor feeling; yet exact every thing that requires the five fenfes in perfection. They expect we fhould know their meaning before they open their lips; yet won't allow we have common underftanding.

HAR. More fhame for 'em. I warrant for all that we can game, run in debt, get in drink, and be as proud and domineering as they for their lives.

WILL. Yes, yes: let them but change places and they would foon find we could rife to their vices, and they could fink to ours, with all the eafe imaginable.

E 2   HAR.

HAR. They have no such notion though, Mr. Williams.

WILL. That is their vanity, Mr. Harry. I have lived with Mr. Delaval ever since he returned from India; and, though he is a good——(*Sees Lucy*) Hay! Surely—It muſt be her! Do you know that young woman, Mr. Harry?

HAR. No: but I have heard a ſtrange ſtory about her.

WILL. Ay!—It is!—What?—I am ſure it is Lucy!—What ſtrange ſtory have you heard?

HAR. Why that ſhe came here late laſt night with a young gentleman, now above, pretending to be his waiting maid.

WILL. With a gentleman!—(*Aſide*) Oh the jilt! Waiting maid to a man? I never heard of ſuch a thing!

HAR. Nor any body elſe.

WILL. (*Aſide*) The deceitful huſſey!

HAR. (*Hears a bell*) That's my lord's bell. I told you, he is never eaſy. I muſt go.

WILL. (*Aſide*) I am glad of it—By all means, Mr. Harry. Good-day——   [*Exit Harry.*

SCENE II.

WILL. Run away with a gentleman! Oh!

LU. (*Coming forward*) I declare, there is Mr. Williams.

WILL. (*Aſide*) What a fool was I to believe ſhe loved me!

LU. (*Aſide*) How my heart beats! Dear, dear! I could wiſh to ſpeak to him—but then if any harm ſhould come of it?

WILL. (*Aſide*) She ſhall not eſcape me!

LU.

Lu. (*Aside*) I fhould like to afk him how he does—But I muft not betray my dear lady. (*Going*)

Will. (*Placing himfelf in her way*) I beg pardon, ma'am.

Lu. (*Aside*) Does not he know me?

Will. I thought I had feen you before; but I find I am miftaken!

Lu. (*Aside*) What does he mean?

Will. You are very like a young woman I once knew.

Lu. (*Aside*) How angry he looks!

Will. But fhe was a modeft pretty behaved perfon; and not an arrant jilt.

Lu. Who is a jilt, Mr. Williams?

Will. One Lucy Langford, that I courted and promifed to marry: but I know better, now.

Lu. You do, Mr. Williams?

Will. I do, madam.

Lu. It is very well, Mr. Williams! It is very well! Pray let me go about my bufinefs!

Will. Oh, to be fure! I have no right to ftop you.

Lu. You have no right to fpeak to me as you do, Mr. Williams.

Will. No, no; ha, ha, ha! I dare fay, I have not.

Lu. (*Her paffions rifing*) No, you have not; and fo I beg you will let me pafs. My miftrefs —I mean—

Will. Ay, ay! You mean, your mafter.

Lu. Do I, fir? Well! Since you pleafe to think fo—fo be it.

Will. All the fervants know it is a man! Would you deny it?

Lu. I deny nothing, Mr. Williams; and, if
you

you are minded to make this an excufe for being
as treacherous as the reft of your fex, (*Keeping down
her fobs*) you are very welcome, Mr. Williams—
I fhall neither die—nor cry, at parting.

WILL. I dare fay not. The young gentleman
above ftairs will comfort you.

Lu. (*Burfts into tears*) It is a bafe falfe ftory.
I have no young gentleman above ftairs, nor below ftairs neither, to comfort me! and you ought
to know me better.

WILL. Did you or did you not come here late
laft night?

Lu. What of that?

WILL. With a young gentleman?

Lu. No. Yes. Don't afk me fuch queftions.

WILL. No! You are afhamed to anfwer them.

SCENE III. MARIA *from the ftaircafe.*

MAR. (*Calls*) Lucy!

Lu. Ma'am! Sir! Coming, fir!

WILL. There! There! I will fee what fort of
a fpark it is, however.

Lu. (*Struggling*) Be quiet, then! Keep away!
You fhan't!

MAR. (*Defcending*) What is the matter? Who
is molefting you?

Lu. (*To Maria*) Go back, fir! Go back!

WILL. I will fee, I am determined!

SCENE IV. DELAVAL *from a room door.*

DEL. Williams!

WILL. I tell you, I will. (*Looking at Maria*)
Hay! Blefs me!

                                   MAR.

MAR. Why, Lucy! Mr. Williams!

WILL. My young lady, as I live!

DEL. Why do not you anfwer, Williams?

WILL. Coming, fir!

MAR. Mercy! It is my brother's voice! What fhall I do?

LU. Hide your face with your handkerchief, ma'am. Pull down your hat.

MAR. Pray do not betray me, Mr. Williams.

LU. If you do, I will never fpeak to you as long as I have breath to draw.

WILL. How betray?

LU. Don't fay you know us. Mind! Not for the world!

[*Exeunt Maria and Lucy up the ftaircafe.*

SCENE V.

DEL. What is it you are about, Williams?

WILL. Nothing, fir.

DEL. What do you mean by nothing? Whom were you wrangling with?

WILL. Me, fir? Wrangling, fir?

DEL. Why are you fo confufed?

WILL. Why, fir, I—I committed a fmall miftake. I was afking—afking after a gentleman that that that proved not to be a gentleman—that is— not not *the* gentleman that I fuppofed.

DEL. Why did you not come back with your meffage?—Have you learnt the addrefs of Sir George?

WILL. Yes, fir: he lives in Upper Grofvenor-ftreet; his name on the door.

DEL. Well, be in the way.—The day fhall not pafs before I fee him. My own wrongs I could forgive. He it feems is preferred; and perhaps

I have

I have no right to complain: But for his injuries to my fifter he fhall render me a dear account.

[*Exit.*

WILL. What can be the reafon of Mifs Delaval's difguife?

Lu. (*Peeping from the top of the ftairs*) Hft! Hft! Mr. Williams!

WILL. Is it you ?—Oh! now I fhall know.

[*Exit up the ftaircafe.*

SCENE VI.

LADY VIBRATE *and* LADY JANE.

LADY V. Really, daughter, I cannot underftand you.

LADY J. No wonder, madam; for I do not half underftand myfelf.

LADY V. Is it poffible you can hefitate? The good humour and complaifance of Sir George might captivate any woman.

LADY J. They are very engaging: but they are dangerous.

LADY V. Which way?

LADY J. His character is too pliant. If others are merry, fo is he: if they are fad, he is the fame. Their joys and forrows play upon his countenance: but, though they may flightly graze, they do not penetrate his heart. Even while he relieves, he fcarcely feels them.

LADY V. Pfhaw! He is a delightful man.

LADY J. I grant he does his utmoft. But it is a folly to be the flave even of an endeavour to pleafe.

LADY V. Ha, ha, ha! Upon my honor, you are a whimfical young lady! Afraid of marrying

4   a man

a man becaufe of his affiduous endeavours to pleafe! As if that were a hufband's failing! You can prefer no fuch accufation againft Mr. Delaval.

Lady J. I own he is of a very different character. Firm and inflexible, he imagines he makes virtue his rule, and reafon his guide.

Lady V. Firm indeed? No, no: ferocious, obftinate, perverfe. Sir George tries to be agreeable, and is fuccefsful: Mr. Delaval has no fear of offending, and does not mifs his aim.

Lady J. Heaven help us! We all have faults and follies enough.

Lady V. Mr. Delaval never was approved by me; and this morning he has infulted your father.

Lady J. Infulted! How do you mean, 'madam? Mr. Delaval is abroad! Has he written?

Lady V. No. He is here.

Lady J. Here! And has he not thought proper to let me know of his arrival?

Lady V. No, no. The haughty gentleman has only thought proper to reproach Lord Vibrate for admitting the pretenfions of Sir George. He is too proud to endure a competitor.

Lady J. Indeed! Such pride is the very way to infure his competitor fuccefs. Infulted my father!

Lady V. I will leave you to judge how deeply when I tell you that, fluctuating and undecided as Lord Vibrate always is, he was fo offended that he pledged his honor in favor of Sir George.

Lady J. Infult my father, and not deign to let me know of his arrival!

Lady V. I hope, when Sir George comes, you will admit him.

Lady J. Certainly, madam; certainly.

F   Lady

LADY V. And that Mr. Delaval will be denied.

LADY J. It seems I need give myself no concern about that : the gentleman will not even take the trouble to send up his name.

LADY V. I am glad you feel it properly.

LADY J. Pardon me, madam. I will not condescend to feel it, in the least. It shall not affect me ; no not for a moment. I had indeed conceived a very different opinion of Mr. Delaval. I am glad I have discovered my error, before it is too late. I could not have believed it possible! But it shall not disturb me. It shall give me no uneasiness. I will keep myself perfectly cool, and unconcerned, and—ungenerous, unfeeling man !

[*Exit.*

S C E N E   VII.

LADY V. She is delightfully piqued, and Sir George will succeed !

SIR G. (*Without*) Are the ladies above ?

FOOT. (*Without*) Yes, sir.

LADY V. I hear him ! The very sound of his voice inspires mirth.

Enter SIR GEORGE.

SIR G. Ah, my dear Lady !

LADY V. I am infinitely glad to see you, Sir George ! You are come at a lucky moment.

SIR G. Is then my fate decided ?

LADY V. It is ! It is !

SIR G. Happy tidings !

LADY V. But first tell me—

SIR G. Any thing ! Every thing ! Speak !

LADY V. Are you not of my opinion?

SIR G.

SIR G. To be sure I am! What is it?

LADY V. That pleasure is the business of life.

SIR G. Oh, beyond all doubt!

LADY V. That inspecting accounts—

SIR G. Is vulgar drudgery!

LADY V. And looking after our affairs—

SIR G. A vile loss of time!

LADY V. That care in the face denotes—

SIR G. The owner a fool!

LADY V. And that sorrow is a very ridiculous thing!

SIR G. Fit only to excite laughter!

LADY V. Why then, Sir George, I am your friend.

SIR G. Ten thousand thousand thanks! But, what says my lord?

LADY V. Would you believe it? He consents, has pledged his honor, and sent the message by me.

SIR G. Rapture! Enchantment!

LADY V. Yes. The reign of pleasure is about to begin!

SIR G. Light, free, and fantastic; dancing an eternal round!

LADY V. No domestic troubles!

SIR G. No grave looks!

LADY V. No serious thoughts!

SIR G. We will never think at all!

LADY V. No cares, no frowns!

SIR G. None, none, by heavens, none! It shall be spring and sunshine all the year!

LADY V. Then our appearance in public!

SIR G. Splendid! Dazzling!—Driving to the opera!

LADY V.

LADY V. Dreffing for Ranelagh!

SIR G. A phaeton to-day!

LADY V. A curricle to-morrow!

SIR G. Dafh over the downs of Piccadilly, defcend the heights of St. James's, make the tour of Pall-mall, coaft Whitehall— .

LADY V. Back again to Bond-ftreet—

SIR G. Scour the fquares, thunder at the doors!

LADY V. How do you do? How do you do? How do you do?

SIR G. And away we rattle, till ftone walls are but gliding fhadows, and the whole world a Galanty fhow.

LADY V. You are a charming man, Sir George! and Lady Jane is yours.

SIR G. My dear lady, your words infpire me! I am all air, fpirit, foul! I tread the milky way, and ftep upon the ftars!

LADY V. But you muft not, before the marriage, talk thus to Lord Vibrate. Silly man! He and you will never agree.

SIR G. Oh yes, but we fhall. I—I—I like his humour!

LADY V. Do you?

SIR G. Prodigioufly! Whenever I am in his company, I am as grave as Good Friday.

LADY V. Indeed!

SIR G. He is full of fage reflection. So am I. Doubtful of every thing. So am I. Anxious for the prefent, provident for the future. So am I. Overflowing with prudential maxims; fententious, fentimental, and folemn. So am I.

LADY V. You fentimental!

SIR G. As grace before meat, in the mouth of an alderman.

Lady V. You folemn!

Sir G. As the black patch on a judge's wig.

Lady V. I muft tell you, Sir George, I hate fentiment.

Sir G. Oh! So do I!

Lady V. Solemnity is all a farce.

Sir G. And thofe that act it buffoons. I know it!

Lady V. I love mirth, pleafantry—

Sir G. Humour, whim, wit, feafting, revelry, fhout, fong, dance, and joke. So do I! So do I! So do I!

Lady V. The very mention of duties and cares makes me fplenetic.

Sir G. Curfe catch duties! I hate them! Give me life, the wide world, the fair fun, and the free air!

Lady V. I fay, give me midnight, the rattling of chariot wheels, and the lighted flambeau!

Sir G. Ay! A rout! A crafh of coaches! A lane of footmen! A blazing ftair-cafe! A fqueeze through the anti-chamber! Card tables! Wax lights! Patent lamps! Bath ftoves and fuffocation! Oh lord! Oh lord!

Lady V. Exquifite! You are a delightful man!

Sir G. Am I?

Lady V. You enter perfectly into all my ideas!

Sir G. Do I?

Lady V. And defcribe them even better than I myfelf can.

Sir G. Oh, my dear lady!

Lady V. Yes, you do.

Sir G. No, no.

Lady V. But then, ha, ha, ha! That you

4 fhould

should be able to fall in with my lord's absurdities
so readily!

SIR G. Nothing more easy. I have one infal-
lible rule to please all tempers. I learnt it of our
friend the Doctor.

LADY V. Sure! What is that?

SIR G. I prove that every body is always in the
right.

LADY V. Prove my husband to be in the right!
Do if you can.

SIR G. My lord loves to be restless, and doubtful, and distressed : he delights in teasing and tor-
menting himself; and why should I interrupt his
pleasures?

LADY V. Ha, ha, ha! Very true.

SIR G. I fall in with his humour. I shew him
how rational it is, afford him new arguments for
discontent, and encourage him to be miserable.

LADY V. Ha, ha, ha! Oh you malicious
divle!

SIR G. My dear lady, you mistake. I do it
from pure compassion. It makes him happy.
Every child delights in the squeaking of its own
trumpet; and shall I have the cruelty to break the
toy? A well bred person is cautious never to
contradict. It is become a very essential requisite
to say Ay, and No, in the most complying manner
possible.

LADY V. Ah, Sir George, you are one of the
dear inimitable few.

SIR G. Only a copy of your charming self.

LADY V. You and I must totally reform our
stupid family. Amusement shall be our perpetual
occupation.

SIR G. Day and night.

LADY V.

LADY V. We will commence with your marriage. It shall be splendid!

SIR G. A feast, a concert, a ball! The whole town shall ring with it!

LADY V. I hate a private wedding. A small select party is my averfion.

SIR G. Oh, nothing is so insipid! Pleasure cannot be calm.

LADY V. I wish to be seen, and heard—

SIR G. And talked of, and paragraphed, and praised, and blamed, and admired, and envied, and laughed at, and imitated!

LADY V. I live but in a crowd.

SIR G. Give me hurry, noise, embarrassment—

LADY V. Confusion, disorder—

SIR G. Tumult, tempest, uproar, elbowing, squeezing, pressing, pushing, squeaking, squalling, fainting!

LADY V. Exquisite! Transporting!

SIR G. You remember I receive masks this evening?

LADY V. Can I forget?

SIR G. You will be there?

LADY V. There? Ay! Though I should come in my coffin.

SIR G. Ha, ha, ha! An excellent idea! I never yet saw a mask in the character of a Memento mori.

LADY V. Ah! Turn about, and you will see a Memento mori without a mask!

SIR G. What, my lord?

LORD V. (Without) I cannot tell. I will confider, and fend an anfwer.

LADY V. Here he comes, to interrupt our delightful dreams: a very antidote to mirth and pleafure.

pleasure. He will give you a full dose of the dismals. But you must stay and speak to him. Remember, his honor is pledged: insist upon that. I pity but cannot relieve you. [*Exit.*

SCENE VIII. *Enter* LORD VIBRATE.

LORD V. I have been too sudden. I ought not to have pledged my honor. This is the consequence of hasty determination: of not doubting before we decide. Shall I never correct myself of that fault? (*Sees Sir George. They look full at each other till Sir George catches the same dismal kind of countenance*) Ah, Sir George! Here am I, brim full of anxiety and turmoil!

SIR G. Alas! Man was born to trouble.

LORD V. Perplexed on every side; thwarted in every plan: no domestic comfort, no friend to grieve with me, no creature to share my miseries.

SIR G. Melancholy case!

LORD V. One crossing me, another blaming me, and my wife driving me mad!

SIR G. Distressing situation!

LORD V. My cares laughed at, my vigilance mocked, my sufferings insulted! And why? Because I am cautious! because I doubt! because I am provident! What is man without money?

SIR G. A fountain without water.

LORD V. A clock without a dial.

SIR G. (*Warming and becoming rapid as he proceeds*) What is it that buys respect, and honor, and power, and privilege, and houses, and lands, and wit, and beauty, and learning, and lords, and commons, and—

LORD V.

LORD V. Why money !—Then the manners of this diffipated age !

SIR G. They are truly fhocking ! They, they, they are abfurd, ridiculous, odious, abominable.

LORD V. And to what do they lead ?

SIR G. To every thing that is horrid ! To lofs of peace, lofs of property, lofs of principle, lofs of refpect, bankruptcy, ruin, contempt, difeafe, and death !

LORD V. *(Afide)* Yes, yes: he's the man ! I do not think I repent——Heaven be praifed, Sir George, you are a man of underftanding ; an economift. You will regulate your family and af-fairs to my heart's content.

SIR G. Oh ! it fhall be my ftudy ! my daily practice ! my duty ! my delight !

LORD V. You make me happy—and yet I cannot but wonder, being fo rational a man, how you and my lady fhould agree fo well.

SIR G. Dear, my lord, why fo ? Women are the moft manageable good creatures upon earth.

LORD V. Women good ?

SIR G. Indubitably : when they are pleafed.

LORD V. So they fay is the devil.

SIR G. The fweet angels deferve to be hu-moured. Their fmiles are fo enchanting ! And, fhould they frown, who can be angry when we know the dear wayward fyrens will only look the more bewitching, as foon as they are out of their pouts ? It is fo delightful to fee the Sun breaking from behind a cloud.

LORD V. Pfhaw ! When a woman begins to grow old—

SIR G. Hufh ! The Sun — The Sun never

grows

grows old. I grant you that formerly there ufed to be old women: but there are none now!

LORD V. Then you think me a fool for being wretched at my wife's thoughtleffnefs, caprice, and impertinence?

SIR G. No, I don't. Every body tells us that wives were born to be the plague of their hufbands.

LORD V. And mine is the greateft of plagues!

SIR G. What is a wife's duty? To obey her lord and mafter. 'Tis her marriage promife, and the law binds her to it. She is the minifter of his pleafures, the handmaid of his wants, his goods, his chattels, his vendible property.

LORD V. Ay: we find the hufband may take the wife to market in a halter.

SIR G. In which I fhould hope he would afterward hang himfelf!

LORD V. My lady thinks of nothing but revelling, and racketing, and turning the world upfide down!

SIR G. 'Tis a great pity.

LORD V. Her tongue is my torment.

SIR G. The perpetual motion! It never ceafes!

LORD V. Then how can you like her company?

SIR G. She is not *my* wife.

LORD V. No, or you would not be fuch good friends. Did fhe fay any thing concerning the marriage?

SIR G. Oh, yes. She delivered your lordfhip's kind meffage.

LORD V. What, that I had pledged my honor?

SIR G. Irrevocably.

LORD V.

Lord V. I was very rash. Hasty resolutions bring long repentance—She insists that the nuptials shall be public!

Sir G. Does she, indeed?

Lord V. For my part, I hate any display of vanity.

Sir G. It is extremely ridiculous! What would our ostentation, pomp, and magnificence be, but advertising ourselves to the world as fools and coxcombs?

Lord V. Is that a rational use of money?

Sir G. Should it not be applied to relieve the aged, comfort the poor, succour the distressed—

Lord V. What?

Sir G. Reward merit, encourage industry, and promote the public good?

Lord V. Promote a farce!

Sir G. Very true: the public good is a farce!

Lord V. The true use of money is to defend our rights——

Sir G. Revenge our wrongs, purchase for the present, provide for the future, secure power, buy friends, bid defiance to enemies, and lead the world in a string!

Lord V. Ay! Now you talk sense. So, if I should consent, the wedding shall be private.

Sir G. Calm: tranquil.

Lord V. No feasting.

Sir G. No dancing: no music: no pantomime pleasures: but all silent, serene, pure, and undisturbed.

Lord V. We will just invite a select party.

Sir G. A chosen few.

Lord V. None but our real and sincere friends.

Sir G. And then we shall be sure the house will hold them.

SCENE

SCENE IX. *Enter* HARRY.

HAR. My lord, the builder defires to know if you will fee him?

LORD V. I am coming. I will be with him in five minutes.

HAR. He fays, he can ftay no longer.

LORD V. Then let him go. I will be with him prefently.

HAR. The lawyers have fent word they are waiting for your lordfhip, at Counfellor Demur's chambers.

LORD V. Very well. There let them wait. The law is flow, and every man ought to be flow who is going to law. Come with me, Sir George. I have fome papers to confult you upon.

HAR. The tradefpeople too are below.

LORD V. Thus it is! I am eternally befieged! I never have a moment to myfelf!

HAR. This is the tenth time they have been here, by your lordfhip's own appointment.

LORD V. What of that?

HAR. They are become quite furly. They all abufe me; and fome of them don't fpare your lordfhip.

LORD V. Do you hear, Sir George?

SIR G. Oh fhocking! Your tradefpeople are a fad unreafonable fet. You cannot convince them that, if we were to keep our appointments, be punctual in our payments, and know what we do want and what we do not, we fhould no longer be perfons of fafhion.

SCENE X. *Enter* THOMPSON.

THOM. I am juft come from the lawyers, my lord. The courts are fitting, their clients waiting, and,

and, if your lordſhip do not go immediately, they
will be gone.

LORD V. Very true; and this laſt opportunity
of ſerving an ejectment will be loſt. I have a thou-
ſand things to attend to. Would you be kind
enough, Sir George, to go and——Hold—No—I
don't know what to do! The eſtate is valuable :
but law is damnable. I may loſe the cauſe : it
may coſt even more than it is worth. Writs of
error! Brought into chancery! Carried up to the
Lords!

SIR G. Then the ſtupidity of juries, the fictions
of law, the chicanery of lawyers, their tricking,
twiſting, turning, lying, wrangling, browbeating,
cajoling!

LORD V. Their frauds, colluſions, perjuries,
robberies!

SIR G. Ay! Detinue, replevin, plea, impar-
lance, replication, rejoinder, rebutter, ſurrejoinder,
ſurrebutter, demurrer——

LORD V. Take breath! We ought both to
demur : for it is the devil's dance, and both Plain-
tiff and Defendant are obliged to pay the piper.

[*Exeunt.*

END OF ACT III.

.

A C T

ACT IV.

SCENE I. *The apartments of* LORD VIBRATE.

LADY JANE, *her* WOMAN, *the* DOCTOR, *and* FOOTMAN.

LADY J. *(To Footman.)*

TELL the young gentleman I wait his pleasure. *(Exit Footman.)* It is very fingular! Men, I believe, do not often travel attended by waiting maids!

DR. Dat is de myftery, my Laty Shane.

LADY J. What can he want to fay to me?

DR. Dat is de more myftery, my Laty Shane. He vas fery mofh young, und fery mofh handfome, und he vas fery mofh make fall in lofe mit you, my Laty Shane.

LADY J. Nonfenfe!

DR. My Laty Shane vas fo full of de beauty dat you vas make fharm efery pody, my Laty Shane! Und as your name vas make mention, my Laty Shane, he vas all fo pale as deaths!

LADY J. *(Afide to her woman.)* You are fure, you fay, Mr. Delaval made enquiries; and fent up his name?

WOM. *(To Lady Jane.)* Law, my lady! Could you think he would not? I faw him before ten o'clock; juft as you fent me where I was kept fo long: and, goodnefs! Had you beheld what a taking he was in! I warrant you, my lady, he afked a hundred and a hundred queftions in a breath; and all about you!

LADY J. Well, go now where I defired you.

WOM. Yes, my lady. [*Exit.*

SCENE II. *Footman returns introducing*
MARIA. *Salute.*

MAR. (*Aside*) Why do I tremble thus?

LADY J. (*To Doctor*) What a charming countenance!

DR. Oh, fery mofh fharming!

LADY J. How prepofleffing his appearance!

DR. Ya: he vas fery mofh poffefs.

Re-enter Footman.

FOOT. Sir George has fent this domino and
mafk, to know if they meet your ladyfhip's approbation.

LADY J. Ha, ha, ha! Italian refinement,
copied after fome Venetian Cicifbeo. Put them
down.

MAR. (*Afide. Regarding the domino and mafk.*)
Here his prefents, and here his affections are now
directed! How fhall I fupport the fcene?

LADY J. You wifh, fir, to fpeak to me.

MAR. (*Faltering*) Embarraffed by the—liberty
—I have taken—

LADY J. Let me requeft you to wave all apology, and tell me which way I can oblige or ferve
you.

MAR. You are acquainted with Sir George—
I—you—Pray pardon me. I am overcome. My
fpirits are—fo agitated—

LADY J. (*Eagerly reaching a chair.*) Sit down,
fir. You are unwell! Blefs me! Doctor!

DR. (*To Lady Jane fignificantly.*) I vas tell my
Laty Shane vat it vas—Here, fair, you fhmell mit
dat elixir; und I fhall make your neck bandt tie
loofe, und—   (*Going to loofen her neckcloth.*)

MAR. (*Alarmed and putting him away.*) Pray
forbear!

DR. (*Aside. Imitating the heaving of the bosom.*) Ah ha! Der Teufel! He vas a vomans!

LADY J. Are you better?

MAR. A moment's air. (*Goes to the window.*)

DR. (*Aside*) Dat vas de someting myftery!

MAR. (*To Lady Jane.*) If you would indulge me a few minutes in private?

LADY J. By all means—Doctor—(*Whispers.*)

DR. Ya, ya, my Laty Shane, I vas unteritandt; und I vas do efery ting as vat fhall make agréable. Dat is my vay——Sair, I vas your mofh oblifhe fery omple fairfant, fair. I vas unterftandt. My Laty Shane, I vas your mofh oblifhe fery omple fairfant, my Laty Shane—(*Aside*) Ah ha! [*Exit.*

SCENE III.

LADY J. Take courage, fir.

MAR. I am unequal to the tafk. This difguife fits ill upon me.

LADY J. What difguife?

MAR. I am not what I feem. I—

LADY J. Speak!

MAR. I am a woman.

LADY J. Heavens!

MAR. Diftreffed——

LADY J. By poverty?

MAR. Oh no. I come to claim your counfel.

LADY J. In what way?

MAR. To prevent mifchief. The fhedding of blood.

LADY J. The fhedding of blood?

SIR G. (*Without.*) I will be with you again prefently, my lady.

MAR. Mercy! It is Sir George! What fhall I do? He muft not fee me! This way—(*Hurries on the domino and mafk.*) Aid me, dear lady, to

9   conceal

conceal myfelf; and excufe conduct which I cannot now explain.

LADY J. Depend· upon me, madam. (*Afide*) This is as unaccountable as it is alarming!

SCENE IV. MARIA *in the back ground.* SIR GEORGE *introduced by a Footman.*

SIR G. I come, my charming Lady Jane, flying and full of bufinefs, to confult you on a thoufand important affairs!

LADY J. Surely! What are they?

SIR G. Upon my foul, I don't know!

LADY J. Heyday!

SIR G. They have every one flipped my memory.

LADY J. Miraculous!

SIR G. Whenever I have the inexpreffible pleafure of enjoying your fmiles, I can think of nothing elfe.

MAR. (*Afide*) Perjured man!

LADY J. My fmiles! Ha, ha, ha! What if I fhould happen to frown?

SIR G. Impoffible! No lowering clouds of difcontent dare ever fhade the heavenly brightnefs of your brow.

MAR. (*Afide*) Oh!

LADY J. Very prettily faid, upon my word. Where did you learn it?

SIR G. From you! 'Tis pure infpiration, and you are my mufe.

LADY J. No, no; 'tis a flight beyond me. I love plain profe.

SIR G. So do I! A mere common place matter of fact man, I! The weather, the time of the

H   day,

day, the history of where I dined laft, the names and titles of the company, the difhes brought to table, the health, ficknefs, deaths, births and marriages of my acquaintance, and fuch like toothpick topics for me! I am as literal in my narratives as any town-crier; and repeat them as often.

Lady J. Yet I fhould wifh to talk a little common fenfe.

Sir G. Oh! So fhould I! I affure you, I am for pros and cons and whys and wherefores. Your Ariftotles, and Platos, and Senecas, and Catos are my delight! I honor their precepts, venerate their cogitations, and adore the length of their beards! which luckily reminds me of the mafquerade. Is my domino to your tafte?

Lady J. Ha, ha, ha! Ancient fages, dominos, and tafte.

Sir G. Did you not notice the colour?

Lady J. Oh! The tafte of a domino is in its colour?

Sir G. Why, no: but there may be meaning.

Lady J. Explain.

Sir G. Mine is faffron.

Lady J. What of that?

Sir G. Cruel queftion! Hymen and his robe.

Lady J. Oh oh!

Mar. *(Afide)* She is pleafed with his perfidy.

Lady J. A very fignificant riddle truly!

Mar. *(Advancing)* Are you fo foon to be married, fir?

Sir G. Blefs me, Lady Jane! What frolickfome gentleman is this? In mafquerade fo early, and my domino!

Mar. Permit me once more to afk, if you are foon to be married?

Sir G.

SIR G. Your queſtion, ſir, is improperly addreſſ-
ed. Put it, if you pleaſe, to that lady.

MAR. (*Aſide to Sir George*) Is that the lady to
whom the queſtion ought to be put?

SIR G. (*Aſide*) What does he mean?—Will
you indulge me, ſir, by taking off that maſk?

MAR. No, ſir.

SIR G. 'Tis mine; and I am induced to claim
it, from the great curioſity I have to ſee your face.

MAR. Do you not adore this lady?

SIR G. (*Aſide*) An odd queſtion!—More than
language can expreſs!

MAR. (*Aſide*) Oh, falſehood!—Then I put
myſelf under her protection.

SIR G. You know guardian angels when you ſee
them. Pray, however, let us become acquainted.

MAR. For what reaſon?

SIR G. 'Twould gratify me. I ſhould like you.

MAR. Oh, no!

SIR G. I certainly ſhould. There is ſomething
of pathos and muſic in your voice, which, which—
I never heard but one to equal it.

MAR. And whoſe voice was that?

SIR G. Oh, that—that was a voice ſo ingenuous,
ſo affectionate, ſo faſcinating!

MAR. But whoſe voice was it?

LADY J. (*Aſide*) What does this mean?

MAR. Tell me, and you ſhall ſee my face.

LADY J. (*Aſide*) Aſtoniſhing!

SIR G. I muſt not—I dare not—I ſhall never
hear it more!

MAR. (*Aſide*) My feelings ſo overpower me I
ſhall betray myſelf. (*To Lady Jane*) Permit me to
retire.

LADY J.

Lady J. You have alarmed and ftrangely moved me! I hope you will return?

Mar. Oh yes; and moft happy to have your permiffion.

Sir G. Why do they whifper? (*To Maria going*) Will you not let me know who you are?

Mar. No.

Sir G. Why?

Mar. Becaufe—I am one you do not love.

[*Exit.*

Sir G. One I do not love!

Lady J. (*Afide*) This is incomprehenfible!

Re-enter Maria *haftily.*

Mar. (*To Lady Jane*) Oh, madam!

Lady J. What more is the matter?

Mar. For your life, do not mention the names of either of thefe gentlemen to the other!

Lady J. What gentlemen?

Mar. He is coming! They do not perfonally know each other. If they fhould, there would be murder! I dare not ftay. For the love of God beware!   '[*Exit mafked as Delaval enters.*

SCENE V.

Sir G. (*Calling*) Harkye, fir, come back! My domino! I fhall want it in an hour or fo—Who have we here?

Del. (*With much agitation of manner*) Your ladyfhip's very humble fervant.

Lady J. Oh! How do you do? How do you do? (*Afide*) Who can that lady be? She knows them both, it feems; and knows their rivalfhip!

Her

Her terror is contagious! Is their hatred so deadly? I shall certainly betray them to each other.

DEL. (*Aside*) What a strange behaviour she puts on! Does she affect to overlook me? (*Observing Sir George*) Who is this?

LADY J. Are you just arrived?

DEL. This very morning: sooner I fear than—than—was desired.

'LADY J. Do you think so? (*To Sir George*) Why don't you go to Lady Vibrate? She is waiting.

SIR G. 'Tis the fate of forty.

LADY J. What?

SIR G. To wait. (*Aside. Eyeing Delaval*) Who can this spark be, that she wants me gone?—Pray what is the name of the youth that has made so free with my domino and mask?

LADY J. I really don't know.

SIR G. Don't know?

LADY J. I can't answer questions at present. I am flurried; out of humour.

DEL. I fear at my intrusion?

LADY J. I wish you had come at another time.

DEL. I expected my visit would be unwelcome: let me request, however, to say a few words.

LADY J. Well, well; another time, I tell you: when I am alone.

SIR G. (*Aside*) Oh ho!

DEL. They were meant for your private ear.

SIR G. (*Aside*) Were they so?

DEL. (*Aside*) By her confusion and his manner, I suspect this to be the base betrayer of my sister's peace: the man whose bare image makes my heart sicken, and my blood recoil.

LADY J.

LADY J. (*Aside*) Will they neither of them go?
—Why do you loiter here, Sir Ge— (*Coughs*)

SIR G. I must stay till the gentleman brings
back my domino and mask, you know. (*Aside*) I'll
not leave them.

DEL. (*Aside*) I am persuaded it is he—Excuse
me, sir : would you indulge me with the favour
of your name ?

SIR G. My name, sir ! My name is—

LADY J. (*Aside to Sir George*) Hush ! Don't
tell it !

SIR G. (*To Lady Jane*) Why not ?

LADY J. I insist upon it !

SIR G. Nay, then—My name, sir, is a very
pretty name. Pray what is yours ?

DEL. (*Aside*) Yes, yes, it must be he—Have
you any reason to be ashamed of it ?

SIR G. Sir ! Did you please to speak ? Upon my
honor, you are a very polite pleasant person.

DEL. (*Aside*) If I should be mistaken—I ac-
knowledge, sir, there is but one man, whose name
I *do* but whose person I do *not* know, to whom that
question would not have been rude in the extreme.
Should you not be that man, I ask your pardon.

SIR G. Should I not ! Sir, that I may be sure I
am not, allow me to ask his name ?

DEL. His name is—

LADY J. (*Screams and sinks on the chair*) Oh !

DEL. Good Heavens !

SIR G. What has happened ?

DEL. Are you ill ?

SIR G. Is it cramp, or spasm ?

DEL. Surely you have not broken a blood ves-
sel ?

SIR G. Shall I run for a physician ?

Lady J. Inftantly.

Sir G. I fly! Yet I muft not leave you!

Lady J. No delay, if you value my life.

Del. Your life! I will go!

Lady J. *(Detaining him)* No, no.

Sir G. I fly! I fly!   [*Exit.*

SCENE VI.   *Enter* Lady Jane's *woman.*

Wom. Dear! my lady, what is the matter?

Lady J. Lead me directly to my own room.

Del. Shall I carry you?

Lady J. No: only give me your arm, and come with me. I want to talk to you. I wifh to hear what you have to fay. *(Afide to her woman)* When Sir George comes back, tell him I am partly recovered, but muft not be difturbed. It is my pofitive order.

Del. *(Afide)* What does fhe whifper?

Lady J. Stay—The Doctor may come in; but not Sir George. Mind, on your life, not Sir George!—Come, fir.

Del. *(Afide)* This fudden change is myfterious. Here is concealment.

Lady J. Come, come.
[*Exeunt Delaval and Lady Jane.*

SCENE VII.

Wom. I purteft, it has put me in fuch a fluster that I am quite all of a twitter!

Enter Sir George *followed by* Dr. Gosterman.

Sir G. Come along, Doctor! Make hafte Where is Lady Jane?

Wom. In her own room.

Sir G.

Sir G. Is fhe worfe?

Wom. No, fir; much better: but fhe muft not be difturbed.

Sir G. Nay, nay, I muft fee her.

Wom. Indeed, fir, I can let nobody in but the Doctor.

Sir G. Why fo? Is not the gentleman I left here now with her?

Wom. I fuppofe fo, fir.

Sir G. And I not admitted?

Wom. On no account whatever.

Sir G. He allowed, and I excluded! Indeed, I fhall attend the Doctor.

Wom. Upon my honor, fir, you muft not.

Sir G. Upon my honor, I will! My rival fhall not efcape me!

Dr. Ah ha! De rifal! Ha, ha, ha! Dat is coot! De young fer dat vas mit Laty Shane vas make you fhealoufy? Ha, ha, ha! Dat is coot! Bote dat is as noting at all. I fhall tell you de fometing myftery. He vas no yentlemans. Ah ha! He vas a vomans.

Sir G. A woman!

Dr. Ya, fair. He vas make acquaintance mit me, und I vas make acquaintance mit him; und he vas make faint, und I vas tie loofe de neck bandt, und den! Ah ha! I vas difcober de mans vas a vomans!

Sir G. You aftonifh me!

Dr. Ya, fair. I vas make aftonifh myfelf.

Wom. Won't you go to my lady, Doctor?

Dr. Ya, my tear. Let me do. Laty Shane is fery pad; und I fhall af de effence, und de cream, und de balfam, und de fyrup, und de electric, und de magnetic, und de mineral, und de vegetable,

table, und de air, und de earfe, und de fea, und all, &c. [*Exit ; gabbling*.

SCENE VIII.

SIR G. I fhould never have fufpected a wo-man! A ftout, tall, robuft figure! And for what purpofe difguife herfelf? That may be worth en-quiry. I will wait and if poffible have another look at the lady.

SCENE IX. *Enter* LORD VIBRATE, *and* MR. THOMPSON.

LORD V. Two hundred and forty pounds! 'Tis a very large fum, Mr. Thompfon.

THOM. So large, my lord, that I have no means of paying it. I muft languifh out my life in a prifon.

LORD V. No, Mr. Thompfon, no: you fhall not do that. I will—And yet—Two hundred— A prifon—I don't know what to fay. If I pay this money for you, I fhall but encourage all around me to run in debt.

THOM. It is a favour too great for me to hope.

LORD V. You are a worthy man, and a prifon is a bad place—I—you—Pray what is your opi-nion, Sir George? Is it not dangerous for a man to have the character of being charitable?

SIR G. No doubt, my lord! It is the very cer-tain way for his houfe to be befieged by beggars!

LORD V. The mafter who pays the debts of one domeftic makes himfelf the debtor of all the reft.

SIR G. He changes a fet of fervants into a fet

I   of

of duns! He firſt encourages them to be extravagant, and then makes it incumbent upon himſelf
to pay for their follies and vices! He not only
bribes them to be idle, and inſolent, but to waſte
his property as well as their own!

Lord V. It is, as you ſay, a very ſerious caſe.
I—I am ſorry for your misfortune, Mr. Thompſon
—very ſorry—but—really—

Sir G. Misfortune! What misfortune?

Lord V. He has fooliſhly been bound for his
ſiſter's huſband; and muſt go to priſon for the
debt.

Sir G. To priſon?

Lord V. You have ſhewn me how dangerous it
would be for me to interfere.

Sir G. Very true: very true.—He has lived
with your lordſhip ſeveral years?

Lord V. He has; and I eſteem him highly.

Sir G. A worthy man, whom it would be no
diſgrace to call your friend?

Lord V. None. Still, however, conſequences
muſt be weighed. I muſt take time to conſider.
'Tis folly to act in a hurry.

Sir G. Very true—caution—caution—Is it a
large ſum?

Lord V. No leſs than two hundred and forty
pounds!

Sir G. Caution is a very excellent thing—Two
hundred and forty—A fine virtue—Two—I would
adviſe your lordſhip to it by all means—hundred
and forty—(*Looks round*) Will you permit me juſt
to write a ſhort memorandum: a bit of a note?
(*Goes to a table*) I muſt ſend to a certain place.
(*Writes*) Excuſe me a moment.

Lord

LORD V. What can be done in this affair, Mr. Thompson?

THOM. Nothing, my lord. I am resigned. When I assisted my brother, I did no more than my duty. Those who lock me up in a prison may, for aught I know, do theirs: yet, though they are at liberty and I shall be confined, I would neither change duties nor hearts with them. (*Going.*)

SIR G. Harkye! Harkye! Mr. Thompson! Will you just desire this to be taken as it is directed? (*Aside to him*) Don't say a word: 'tis a draft on my banker. Discharge your debt; and be silent—You are very right, my lord: we cannot be too considerate; lest, by mistaken benevolence, we should encourage vice.

THOM. Sir George! My lord!

SIR G. Why now will you not oblige me, Mr. Thompson? Pray let that be delivered as it is directed. You surely will not deny me such a favor—For you know, my lord, if we give—

THOM. Indeed, I—

SIR G. Will you begone? Will you begone? (*Pushes him kindly off,*—If we give without—without—

LORD V. Poor fellow! I suppose he is afraid of being taken.

SIR G. Oh! Is that it?—If we give, I say, with—too—Pshaw! I have lost the thread of my argument.

LORD V. I must own, this is a dubious case. Perhaps I ought to pay the money. (*Calls*) Mr. Thompson!—I don't think I ought to let him go to prison. What shall I do, Sir George?

SIR G. Whatever your lordship thinks best.

LORD V. But there is the difficulty!—Mr. Thompfon! He is gone. How foolifh this is now! (*As he is going off*) Harry! Run after Mr. Thompfon, and call him back. One would think a man going to prifon would like me be wife enough to doubt, and take time to confider of it.

[*Exit.*

SCENE X. *Enter* LADY VIBRATE.

LADY V. I affure you, Sir George, I am very angry. I have been waiting an age, expecting you would come and give your opinion on my mafquerade drefs.

SIR G. Why did not your ladyfhip put it on?

LADY V. On, indeed? It has been on and off twenty times! I have fent it to have fome alteration. Befide it is growing late: mafks will be calling in on you, in their way to the Opera-houfe, and you not at home to receive them!

SIR G. I afk ten thoufand pardons, but you know I am the moft thoughtlefs creature on earth.

LADY V. So I would have you. Were you like the fober punctual Mr. Delaval, I fhould hate you. But then—

SCENE XI.

DELAVAL *returning from* LADY JANE'S *apartment.*

LADY V. (*Afide*) Here the wretch comes!

SIR G. (*Afide*) So, fo! now I fhall interrogate the lady. She has a very mafculine air! (*Delaval bows to Lady Vibrate*) A tolerable bow that, for a woman!

LADY V. (*Afide*) He wifhes, I fuppofe, to fer-
monize

4

monize me: but I fhall not give him an opportunity—Are you coming, Sir George?

DEL. (*Afide*) Ha!

SIR G. I will follow your ladyfhip in a minute.

DEL. (*Afide*) I was right! It is he!

SIR G. (*Afide*) She eyes me very ferocioufly!

LADY V. I fhall juft call in upon you: or, if
not, we fhall meet afterward. I expect you to be
very whimfical and fatiric upon all my friends;
fo pray put on your beft humour. Grave airs, you
know, are my averfion. [*Exit.*

SCENE XII.

DEL. (*Afide*) That was intended for me. Now
for my gentleman.

SIR G. (*Afide*) She really has a very fierce
look! A kind of threatening phyfiognomy; and
would make no bad Grenadier.

DEL. I underftand, your name is Sir George
Verfatile?

SIR G. (*Afide*) A bafs voice too!—At your fer-
vice, fir; or madam; I really cannot tell which.

DEL. Cannot!

SIR G. No, I cannot upon my foul! (*Afide*) A
devilifh black chin!

DEL. I have an account to fettle with you, fir.

SIR G. Have you? (*Afide*) What the plague
can fhe mean?

DEL. When can I find you at leifure, and alone?

SIR G. Alone?

DEL. Yes, fir; alone.

SIR G. Muft this account then be privately
fettled, madam?

DEL.

DEL. Madam!

SIR G. I beg your pardon! *Sir*, since you prefer it.

DEL. If you know me, sir, your insolence is but a confirmation of the baseness of your character!

SIR G. I beg a million of pardons! I really do not know you.

DEL. Then, sir, when you do, you will find cause to be a little more serious.

SIR G. (*Aside*) What a Joan of Arc it is! There is danger she should knock me down.

DEL. Be pleased to name your time.

SIR G. (*Aside*) Zounds! She insists upon a tête-à-tête!—I hope you will be kind enough to excuse me, but I am just now so pressed for time that I have not a moment to spare. Company is waiting. I must begone to the masquerade. You I presume are for the same place, and are ready dressed. I am your most obedient—

DEL. (*Seizing him*) Sir, I insist upon your naming an hour, to-morrow; and an early one.

SIR G. Why, what the plague!—Here must be some mistake! Permit me to ask, do you know Dr. Gosterman?

DEL. Yes, sir.

SIR G. Was you not just now in danger of fainting?

DEL. Faint? I faint!

SIR G. It would I think be a very extraordinary thing! But so he told me: with other particulars.

DEL. Absurd! Dr. Gosterman has not seen me for several months.

SIR G. He said, sir, you were a woman; and
perhaps,

perhaps, from that error, I may have unconfci-
oufly provoked you to behaviour which would elfe
have been rather ftrange.   Have I given you any
other offence ?

DEL. Yes, fir; a mortal one.

SIR G. Mortal !

DEL. And mortal muft be the atonement.

SIR G. If fo, the fooner the better.   Let it be
immediately.

DEL. No.   I have ferious concerns to fettle.
So have you !   'Tis time you fhould think of
things very different from mafquerading.   Name
your hour to-morrow morning ; then, take an
enemy's advice, retire to your clofet, and make
your will.

SIR G. To whom am I indebted for this high
menace, and this haughty warning ?   Your name,
fir ?   .

DEL. That you fhall know when next we meet :
not before.

SIR G. What age are you, fir ?

DEL. Age !

SIR G. Such peremptory heroes are not ufually
long lived.

DEL. You are right, fir ; my life is probably
doomed to be fhort.   But this is trifling.   Name
your hour.

SIR G. At ten to-morrow morning.

DEL. The very time I could wifh.   I will be
with you at your own houfe, inform you who I
am, and, then—

SIR G. So be it.—   [Excunt.

SCENE

SCENE XIII. *Changes to the house of* Sir
    George. *A suite of apartments richly decorated
    and numerous masks: some dancing; others passing
    and repassing.*

Sir George *and* Lady Vibrate *advance, un-
    masked.*

Lady V. What is the matter with you, Sir
George? You are suddenly become as dull and
almost as intolerable as my lord himself.

Sir G. I own, I had something on my spirits.
But it is gone. Your ladyship's vivacity is an antidote to splenetic fits.

Lady V. Oh, if you are subject to fits of the
spleen, I renounce you.

Sir G. No, no! Heigho! Ha, ha, ha! Let
me go merrily down the dance of life!

Lady V. Ay! or I will not be your partner.

Sir G. As for recollections, retrospective anx-
ieties, and painful thoughts, I I I hate them.
They shall not trouble me. For if a man, you
know, were to be sprung on a mine to-morrow,
ha, ha, ha! it were folly to let that trouble him
to-day.

Lady V. Sprung on a mine? You talk wildly!

Sir G. True. I am a wild unaccountable non
descript. I am any thing, every thing, and soon
may be—

Lady V. What?

Sir G. Nothing. Strange events are possible;
and possible events are strange.

Lady V. Come, come, cast off this disagree-
able humour; and join the masks.

Sir G. With all my heart. A mask is an ex-
                                                                    cellent

cellent utenfil; and may be worn with a naked face.

LADY V. (*Retiring*) Why don't you come? You ufed to be all compliance.

SIR G. So I fear I always fhall be. 'Tis my worft virtue. Call it a vice, if you pleafe; and perhaps it is even then my worft.

LADY V. I really do not comprehend you.

SIR G. No wonder. Man is an incomprehenfible animal! But no matter for that. We will be merry ftill fay I—at leaft till to-morrow.

LADY V. (*Joins the mafks*) Yonder is Lady Jane.

SCENE XIV.

SIR G. Nay then, I am on the wing!

MARIA (*Advancing*) Whither?

SIR G. Ah! Have I found you again? So much the better! I have been thinking of you this half hour.

MAR. Ay? That muft have been a prodigious effort?

SIR G. What?

MAR. To think of one perfon for fo great a length of time.

SIR G. True. Were you my bittereft enemy, you could not have uttered a more galling truth. I am glad I have met with you, however.

MAR. So am I. 'Tis my errand here.

SIR G. You now, I hope, will let me fee your face?

MAR. I might, perhaps, were it but poffible to fee your heart.

SIR G. No, no: that cannot be. I have no heart.

MAR. I am forry for it!

K   SIR G

SIR G. So am I. But come, I wish to be better acquainted with you.

MAR. And I wish you to be better acquainted with yourself. You know not half your own good qualities.

SIR G. Ha, ha, ha! My good qualities? Heigho!

MAR. Your fame is gone abroad! Your gallantry, your free humour, your frolics in England and Italy, your—Apropos: I am told, Lady Jane is captivated by the ardour and delicacy of your passion! Is it true?

SIR G. Are you an inquisitor?

MAR. Are you afraid of inquisitors?

SIR G. Yes.

MAR. I believe you.

SIR G. You may. Keep me no longer in this suspense. Let me know who you are?

MAR. An old acquaintance.

SIR G. Of mine?

MAR. Of one who was formerly your friend.

SIR G. Whom do you mean?

MAR. You must have been a man of uncommon worth; for I have heard him bestow such praises upon you that my heart has palpitated if your name was but mentioned!

SIR G. Of whom are you talking?

MAR. Lord! that you should be so forgetful! That can only have happened since you became a person of fashion: for no man once remembered his friends better. It is true, they were then useful to you.

SIR G. Sir, I—Be warned! Pursue this no farther.

MAR. You little suspected at that time you were on the eve of being a wealthy baronet. Oh no!

no! And to fee how kind and grateful you were to thofe who loved you! No one would have believed you could fo foon have become a perfect man of the mode ; and with fo polite and eafy an indifference fo entirely have forgotten all your old acquaintance! I dare fay you fcarcely remember the late Colonel Delaval.

Sir G. Sir!

Mar. His daughter too has utterly flipped your memory?

Sir G. I infift on knowing who you are!

Mar. How different it was when, your merit neglected, your fpirits depreffed, and your poverty defpifed, you groaned under the oppreffion of an unjuft and felfifh world! How did your drooping fpirits revive by the foftering fmiles of the man who firft noticed you, took you to his houfe and heart, and adopted you as his fon! Poor Maria! Silly girl, to love as fhe did! Where is fhe?

Sir G. This is not to be endured!

Mar. What was her offence? You became a baronet! Ay! True, that was her crime. Yet, when your fortunes were low, it was not imputed to you as guilt.

Sir G. (*Afide.*) Damnation!

Mar. Are your new friends more affectionate than your old? Fortune fmiles, and fo do they. Poor Maria! Has Lady Jane ever heard her name? Will you invite her to your wedding? (*Her voice continually faltering.*) Do. She fhould have been your bride: then let her be your bride maid—She is greatly altered—She will be lefs beautiful—now—than her fair rival. Her birth is not quite fo high—but—if a—heart—a heart—

a heart

a heart——(*Struggling with her feelings sinks into Sir George's arms, and her mask falls off*)

SIR G. Heavens and earth! 'Tis she! Help! 'Tis Maria! Who waits?

SCENE XV. *Enter* LADY JANE.

LADY J. What is the matter?

SIR G. Help! Help!——Salts! Hartshorn! —Water! Help!

LADY J. Bless me! This lady again.

SIR G. Is she then known to you?

LADY J. No! Who is she?

SIR G. Quick! Quick!

LADY J. Nay but, tell me?

SIR G. I cannot! Must not!

LADY J. Must not?

SIR G. Dare not!—She revives; and, to my confusion, will soon tell you herself. Maria! Are you better, Maria?

MAR. I am very faint.

LADY J. My carriage is at the door. Will you trust yourself to me?

MAR. Oh yes. I am weak—Very weak, and very foolish! But I shall not long disturb your happiness. I hope soon to be past that.

SIR G. Past! Oh Maria!—I—have no utterance—Lady Jane, you will presently know of me what to know of myself is—Oh!—No matter. Not then for my sake but for pity, for the love of suffering virtue, be careful of this lady; whom when you know, as soon you must, you will despise and abhor the lunatic, the wretch, that could ——Maria—I—I——   [*Exit abruptly.*

SCENE

SCENE XVI. *Enter* DELAVAL.

DEL. What is the matter? Any accident? Was not that Sir George?——Good God! My fister!

LADY J. Your fister!

DEL. How comes this? Why this drefs? And with that apoftate! that wretch! Speak, Maria!

MAR. I cannot.

LADY J. Mr. Delaval, be more temperate. Your fister's fpirits and health ought not to be trifled with by your violence. I do not know, though I think I guefs, her ftory. I hope you have a brother's tendernefs for her?

DEL. That fhall be fhortly feen. A few hours will fhew how dear fhe is to my heart.

LADY J. I fear you cherifh bad paffions: fuch as I never can love, and never will fhare.

DEL. Well, well, Lady Jane, that is not to be argued now. I am a man, and fubject to the miftakes of man. There are feelings which can and feelings which cannot be fubdued. I muft run my courfe, and take all confequences.

MAR. Oh God! In what will they end?

LADY J. No more of this, Mr. Delaval. Come with me: lead your fister to my carriage. She fhall be under my care. She can infpire thofe fympathies which your too ftubborn temper feems to defpife.

DEL Indeed, indeed, you wrong me! [*Exeunt.*

END OF ACT IV.

ACT V.

SCENE I. MARIA *in her proper dress,* LADY JANE *and* LUCY, FOOTMEN *waiting. Breakfast equipage on the table.*

LADY JANE.

REMOVE those things. We have done.

　　　　　　　　　　[*Exeunt Footmen.*

MAR. What is it o'clock?

LU. Just struck ten, ma'am.

LADY J. Lady Vibrate is a sad rake! She did not leave the masquerade till five this morning.

MAR. And Sir George not there!

LADY J. After the discovery of last night, could you suppose he would be seen revelling at such a place?

MAR. I dread another and more horrible cause! My brother!

LADY J. Mr. Delaval, you know, slept in this house.

MAR. But he has been out these two hours!

LU. What then, ma'am? Is not Mr. Williams on the watch? You know, ma'am, you may trust Mr. Williams with your life.

MAR. If all were safe, he would be back.

LADY J. Pray calm your spirits.

MAR. Nay, nay, but Mr. Williams must have been here before this, if something fatal had not happened!

LU. I am sure, ma'am, you frighten me to death!

LADY J. (*Aside*) Her terrors are but too well founded!

MAR. (*Footsteps without*) What noise is that?

　　　　　　　　　　　　　　　　　LU.

Lu. Blefs me!

Lady J. See who it is!

Lu. (*After ope.ing the door*) Law, ma'am! I declare it is Mr. Williams!

SCENE II. *Enter* Williams.

Lu. Well, Mr. Williams! Every thing is right: is not it? All is as it fhould be?

Will. That is more than I know.

Mar. Why then the worft is paft.

Will. No, ma'am: I can't fay that, either.

Lady J. Nay but, what news do you bring? Speak.

Will. Why you know my mafter laft night made enquiries how to find the chambers of Counfellor Demur: fo, when he went out this morning, I obferved your directions and followed him. He went to the Counfellor's, in Lincoln's Inn; and there I left him and hurried away to Sir George's, to enquire and hear all I could: though it was rather unlucky that I was not acquainted in the family.

Lady J. Did not you make ufe of my name?

Will. Oh yes, my lady. Befide, fervants your ladyfhip knows are not fo fufpicious as their maf-ters: they foon become friendly together: fo in five minutes Sir George's valet and I were on as intimate a footing as we could wifh.

Mar. And what did he fay? Tell me.

Will. Why, ma'am, he faid that Sir George did not leave his own houfe laft night, after the fainting of the young gentleman.

Lu. That was you, you know, ma'am.

Will. And, what is more, that he did not go to bed; but walked up and down the room till daylight

daylight in the morning; and then called I don't know how often to warn the servants that he should not be at home to any body whatever, except to a strange gentleman.

MAR. My brother!

WILL. Why yes, ma'am, according to the description, it could be nobody else.

LADY J. And at what hour was Mr. Delaval to be there?

WILL. (*Aside*) Zooks! I forgot to ask—That, that, my lady, I did not learn. So, this being all the servants told me, I ran post haste to make my report to you.

MAR. The worst I foreboded will happen!

LADY J. What can be done?

WILL. Perhaps it will be best for me to go back to Sir George's, wait for the arrival of my master, and, if he should come, hasten away as fast as I can to inform you of it.

LU. That is a good thought, Mr. Williams! Is not it, madam? A very good thought, indeed! Don't you think it is, my lady?

LADY J. I know not what we can do better.

MAR. Nay but, while Williams is bringing us the intelligence, every thing we most dread may happen.

LU. Dear! So it may!

WILL. Suppose then, madam, I should stay at my post; and dispatch Sir George's valet to you with the news?

LU. Well, that is the best thought of all!! I am sure you will own it is, madam.

MAR. I know not what to think.

LADY J. We must resolve; or, while we are deliberating—

MAR.

MAR. Merciful God! Run, Williams! Fly! Save my brother! Save Sir George!

LADY J. Succeed but in this, and command all we have to give.

WILL. I will do my best.

LU. That I am sure he will. [*Exeunt.*

SCENE III. *Changes to the house of* SIR GEORGE. —SIR GEORGE *walking in perturbation of mind. After some time he looks at his watch.*

SIR G. He will soon be here—Five minutes— but five minutes and then—(*Walks again, throws himself on a sofa, takes up a book, tosses it away and rises*) What is man's first duty? To be happy. Short sighted fool! The happiness of this hour is the misery of the next! (*Again walks and looks at his watch*) What is life? A tissue of follies! Inconsistencies! Joys that make reason weep, and sorrows at which wisdom smiles. Pshaw! There is not between ape and oyster so ridiculous or so wretched a creature as man. (*Walks*) Oh Maria! (*Again consulting his watch*) I want but a few seconds. My watch perhaps is too fast. (*Rings*)

Enter Footman.

SIR G. Has nobody yet been here?

FOOT. No, sir.

SIR G. 'Tis the time to a minute. (*Loud knocking*) Fly! If it be the person I have described, admit him. [*Exit Footman.*

SIR G. Now let the thunder strike!

SCENE IV.   DELAVAL *introduced.   They salute:*

SIR G. Good morning, fir!

DEL. You recollect me ?

SIR G. Perfectly.

DEL. 'Tis well.

SIR G. I have been anxious for your coming.
Your menace lives in my memory; and I shall be
glad to know the name of him who has threatened
such mortal enmity.

DEL. A little patience will be neceffary.   I
muft preface my proceedings with a fhort ftory.

SIR G. I fhall be all attention.   Pleafe to be
feated.   Wave ceremony, and to the fubject—
(They fit) Now, fir.

DEL. About fix years ago, a certain youth came
up from college; poor, and unprotected.   He
was a fcholar, pleafing in manner, warm and generous of temper, of a refpectable family, and
feemed to poffefs the germ of every virtue.

SIR G. Well, fir.

DEL. Hear me on : my praifes will not be te-
dious.   Chance made him known to a man who
defired to cherifh his good qualities; and the
purfe, the experience, and the power of his benefactor, fuch as they were, he profited by to the
utmoft.   Received as a fon, he foon became dear
to the family : but moft dear to the daughter of
his friend; whofe tender age and glowing affections
made her apt to admire the virtues fhe heard her
father fo ardently praife, and encourage.   You are
uneafy ?

SIR G. Be pleafed to continue.

DEL. The affiduities of the youth to gain her
heart

heart were unabating; and his pretenfions, poor and unknown as he then was, were not rejected. The noble nature of his friend fcorned to make his poverty his crime. Why do you bite your lip? Was it not generous?

SIR G. Sir!

DEL. *(Firmly)* Was it not?

SIR G. Certainly! Nothing could—equal the —generofity.

DEL. The health of his benefactor was declining faft; and the only thing required of the youth was that he fhould qualify himfelf for the cares of life, by fome profeffion. He therefore entered a ftudent in the Temple; and the means were furnifhed by his protector, till the end was obtained. Was not this friendfhip?

SIR G. It was.

DEL. The lady, almoft a child when firft he knew her, increafed in grace and beauty fafter than in years. Sweetnefs and fmiles played upon her countenance. She was the delight of her friends, the admiration of the world, and the coveted of every eye. Lovers of fortune and fafhion contended for her hand: but fhe had beftowed her heart—had beftowed it on a — Sit ftill, fir; I fhall foon have done. I am coming to the point. Five years elapfed; during which the youth received every kindnefs friendfhip could afford, and every proof chafte affection had to give. Thefe he returned with promifes and proteftations that feemed too vaft for his heart. I would fay for his tongue—Are you unwell, fir?

SIR G. Go on with your tale.

DEL. His benefactor, feeling the hand of death fteal on, was anxious to fee the two perfons deareft

L 2

to his heart happy before he expired; and the
marriage was determined on, the day fixed, and
the friends of the family invited. The intended
bridegroom appeared half frantic with his ap-
proaching blifs. Now, fir, mark his proceeding.
In this fhort interval, by fudden and unexpected
deaths, he becomes the heir to a title and large
eftate. Well! Does he not fly to the arms of
his languifhing friend? Does he not pour his
new treafures and his tranfports into the lap of
love? Coward and monfter!

Sir G. (*Both ftarting up*) Sir!

Del. Viler than words can paint! Having
robbed a family of honor, a friend of peace, and
an angel of every human folace, he fled, like a
thief, and concealed himfelf from immediate contempt and vengeance in a foreign country. But
contempt and vengeance have at length overtaken
him: they befet him: they face him at this inftant.
The friend he wronged is dead: but the fon of
that friend lives, and I am he.

Sir G. 'Tis as I thought!

Del. You are—I will not defile my lips by
telling you what you are.

Sir G. I own that what I have done—

Del. Forbear to interrupt me, fir. You have
nothing to plead, and much to hear. Firft fay,
did my fifter, by any improper conduct, levity of
behaviour, or fault or vice whatever, give you
juft caufe to abandon her?

Sir G. None! None! Her purity is only ex-
ceeded by her love.

Del. Then how, barbarian, how had you the
heart to difgrace the family and endanger the life
of a woman whofe fanctified affection would have
embraced

embraced you in poverty, peſtilence, or death ;
and who, had ſhe poſſeſſed empires, would have
beſtowed them with an imperial affection ?

Sir G. Sir, if you aſk, Have I committed er-
rors ? call them crimes if you will, Yes. If you
demand, Will I juſtify them ? No. If you re-
quire me to atone for them, here is my heart : you
have wrongs to revenge, ſtrike ; and, if you can,
inflict a pang greater than any it yet has known.

Del. Juſtice is not to be diſarmed by being
braved. To the queſtion. It can be no part of
your intention, and certainly not of mine, that
you ſhould marry my ſiſter. Something very different muſt be done.

Sir G. What ? Name it ?

Del. You muſt give me an acknowledgment,
written and ſigned by yourſelf, that you have
baſely and moſt diſhonorably injured, inſulted and
betrayed Maria Delaval : and this paper, immediately as I leave your houſe, I ſhall publiſh in
every poſſible way ; till my ſiſter ſhall be ſo ap-
peaſed, and honor ſo ſatiated, that vengeance itſelf
ſhall cry, Hold !

Sir G. Written by me ! Publiſhed ! No. I
will ſign no ſuch paper.

Del. So I ſuppoſed ; and the alternative fol-
lows. Here I am : nor will I quit you, go where
you will, till you ſhall conſent to retire with me to
ſome place from which one of us muſt never return. Should I be the victor, flight, bániſhment
from my native country, and the bittereſt recollections of the villanies of man, muſt be the fate of
me and my ſiſter. If I fall, you then may tri-
umph and ſhe languiſh and die unrevenged. This,

or

or the written acknowledgment. Confider, and chufe.

Sir G. What can I anfwer? The paper you fhall not have. My life you are welcome to: take it.

Del. Have you not brought difgrace enough on my family? Would you make me an affaffin? My fifter and my father loved you. Let me, if poffible, feel fome little return of refpect for you.

Sir G. Having wronged the fifter, would you have me murder the brother? Already the moft guilty of men, would you make me the worft of fiends? Though an enemy, be a generous one.

Del. Plaufible fophift! The paper, fir: or, man to man and arm to arm, clofe the fcene of my difhonor, or your own. The written acknowledgment. Determine. (*Walks away and views the pictures*)

Sir G. (*Apart*) Why, ay! 'Tis come home! I have fought it, deferved it, 'tis fallen, and the rock muft crufh the reptile!—Then welcome ruin. The fword muft decide. (*Goes to take his fword, but ftops*) The fword? What! Betray the fifter and affaffinate the brother? Oh God! And fuch a brother! Stern, but noble minded: indignant of injury, peerlefs in affection, and proud of a fifter whom the world might worfhip; but whom I, worthlefs wretch, in levity and pride of heart, have abandoned. (*Aloud*) Mr. Delaval!

Del. Have you refolved to fign?

Sir G. Hear me.

Del. The written acknowledgment!

Sir G. My behaviour to your fifter is—what I cannot endure to name—'Tis hateful! 'Tis—infamous!

famous! My obligations to your moſt excellent
father, the reſpect you have inſpired me with, and
my love for Maria—

DEL. Inſolent! Inſufferable meanneſs! The
paper, Sir!

SIR G. Angry though you are, Mr. Delaval,
you muſt hear me. I ſay, my love, my adora-
tion of Maria has but increaſed my guilt. It has
made me dread her contempt. I durſt not face
the angel whom I had ſo deeply injured.

DEL. Artifice! Evaſion! Cowardice!—Your
ſignature!

SIR G. *(Snatching up his ſword from the table)*
You ſhall have it. Follow me.

DEL. Fear me not.

SIR G. *(Stopping ſhort)* Hold, Mr. Delaval.
Juſtice is on your ſide. If your firmneſs be not
a ſavage ſpirit of revenge, if you do not thirſt for
blood, you will feel my only reſource will be to
fall on your ſword. I cannot lift my arm againſt
you.

DEL. Then ſign the acknowledgment.

SIR G. Can you in the ſpirit even of an enemy
aſk it? Do you not already deſpiſe me enough?
Think for a moment: am I the only man that ever
erred? Is it ſo wonderful that a giddy youth,
whoſe habitual failing was compliance, by ſudden
accident elevated to the pinnacle of fortune, ſur-
rounded by proud and ſelfiſh relations of whoſe
approbation I was vain, is it ſo ſtrange that I
ſhould be overpowered by their dictates, and yield
to their intreaties? Your friendſhip or my death is
now the only alternative. Suppoſe the latter: will
it honor you among men? At the man of blood
the heart of man revolts! Will it endear you to
Maria?

Maria? Kind forgiving angel, and hateful to myself as her affection makes me, I laft night found that affection ftill as ftrong, ftill as pure, as in the firft hour of our infant loves. Lady Jane—

DEL. Forbear to name her! 'Tis profanation from your lips! No more cafuiftry! No fub-terfuge! The paper!

SIR G. Can no motives—

DEL. None!

SIR G. My future life, my foul, fhall be de-voted to Maria.

DEL. The paper!

SIR G. Obdurate man! *(Reflects a moment)* You fhall have it. *(Goes to the table to write, dur-ing which Delaval remains deep in thought and much agitated)* Here, fir! fince *you* will not be generous, let *me* be juft. 'Tis proper I remove every taint of fufpicion from the deeply wronged Maria.

DEL. *(Reads with a faltering voice)* " I George " Verfatile, once poor and dependent, fince vain " fickle and faithlefs, do under my hand acknow- " ledge I have perfidioufly—broken my pledged " promife—to the moft deferving—lovely—and *(Begins in much agitation to tear the paper.)*

SIR G. Mr. Delaval?

DEL. Damn it—I can't—I can't fpeak. Here! Here! *(Striking his bofom.)*

SIR G. Mr. Delaval?

DEL. My brother!

SIR G. *(Falls on his neck)* Can it be? My friend!

DEL. This ftubborn temper — always in ex-tremes! The tiger, or the child.

SIR G. Oh no! 'Twas not to be forgiven! Beft of men!

DEL.

Del. Well, well: we are friends.

Sir G. Everlaftingly! Brothers!

Del. Yes; brothers.

SCENE V. *Enter* Williams *in great hafte.*

Will. Sir!

Del. How now?

Will. I beg your pardon, but Lady Jane and your fifter are below. They infift on coming up, and the fervants are afraid to—

Sir G. Maria! Let us fly! [*Exeunt.*

SCENE VI. *The apartments of* Lord Vibrate.

Lady Vibrate *and the* Doctor.

Dr. Ya, my coot laty: dat vas efery vordt fo true as vat I fay. I vas difcober it vas a vomans; und Sair Shorge, und my Laty Shane, und de vaiting vomans vas difcober to me all as vat I fay more.

Lady V. Ay, ay! That was the reafon Sir George was not at the mafquerade.

Dr. Ya, my coot laty.

Lady V. I obferved he was in a ftrange moody humour.

Dr. My Lordt Fiprate vas fery mofh amazement, ven I vas make him difcober all as vat I vas make difcober mit my coot laty.

Lady V. Sir George has behaved very improperly.

SCENE VII. *Enter* Lord Vibrate.

Lord V. So, fo, fo! All I foreboded has come to pafs! The day is flipped away, a new one is

M here,

here, and every poſſibility of recovering the eſtate
is gone!

LADY V. Ha, ha, ha!

LORD V. Do you laugh?

LA Y V. Ha, ha, ha! I do, indeed!

LORD V. Is your daughter's loſs the ſubjeƈt of
your mirth?

LADY V. Ha, ha, ha! No, no; not her loſs,
but your poſitive determination to prove I did not
know you! Ha, ha, ha! When I told you that
even that motive would not be ſtrong enough, how
you ſtormed! "But it will, my lady! But it
won't, my lord! I ſay it will, my lady! I ſay
it won't, my lord!" Ha, ha, ha! Will you
believe that I know you now?

LORD V. What ſhall I do? Adviſe me, Doƈtor.

DR. I vas adfice, my coot Lordt, dat you ſhall
do efery ting as vat you pleaſe.

LADY V. Ay, think: aſk advice. Ha, ha, ha!
Now that you can do nothing, the enquiry will be
very amuſing.

SCENE VIII. *Enter* THOMPSON.

LORD V. Well, Thompſon, what ſays Coun-
ſellor Demur? Has the time abſolutely elapſed?

THOM. Abſolutely, my lord.

LADY V. How wiſely your lordſhip doubts,
before you decide! Hay, Doƈtor?

THOM. I have good news, nevertheleſs.

LORD V. Good news? Speak! Of what kind?

THOM. The honeſty of the oppoſite party.

LORD V. What, the holder of the land?

THOM. Yes, my lord.

LORD V. Which way? Explain!

THOM.

THOM. He has engaged to Mr. Demur, I being prefent, that, if your lordfhip will only fhew the legality of your late title, he will refign the eftate.

LORD V. Is it poffible?

LADY V. It cannot be! The laft purchafer is in India.

THOM. The laft purchafer is dead; and it has defcended to one whom you, my lord and lady, little fufpect to be its poffeffor.

LORD V. Who?

LADY V. Who?

THOM. Mr. Delaval.

LADY V. Mr. Delaval!

LORD V. Mr. Delaval refign it on exhibiting the legality of my title?

THOM. He will, my lord.

LORD V. Did he make no conditions?

THOM. None.

LORD V. What, did he not mention Lady Jane?

THOM. Her name did efcape his lips; but rifing paffion, and, if I rightly read his heart, emotions of the moft delicate fenfibility immediately clofed them: as if he would not endure the love he bore her to be profaned by any the flighteft femblance of barter and fale.

LORD V. What do you fay to that, Lady Vibrate? What do you fay to that?

LADY V. The proceeding is honorable, I own.

LORD V. Did I not always tell you Mr. Delaval was a man of honor?

LADY V. You tell me, my lord? Why you were going to challenge him yefterday morning!

LORD V. He is no fuch weathercock as your favorite, Sir George.

M 2

LADY V.

LADY V. You miftake: Sir George is no favorite of mine. Is he, Doctor?

DR. Dat vas all yuft as vat you fay, my coot laty.

LORD V. What, he did not come to make a
buffoon of himfelf, for your diverfion, at the mafquerade laft night! Hay, Doctor?

DR. Dat vas all yuft as vat you fay, my coot
lordt.

LADY V. His perfidious treatment of Mifs Delaval is unpardonable.

DR. Dat vas pad! Fery pad, inteet!

LORD V. Ay ay! He has plenty of words, but
he has no heart.

DR. Dat is pad! Fery pad inteet!

THOM. Pardon me, my lord: Sir George may
have committed miftakes, but to the goodnefs of
his heart I am a witnefs.

LADY V. You?

LORD V. How fo?

THOM. By his benevolence, I was yefterday re-
lieved from the difgrace and the horrors of a prifon.

LORD V. Indeed!

LADY V. Which way?

THOM. He paid a debt, which, had I been confined, I never could have difcharged; and, for this
unexpected act of humanity, he would not fuffer fo
much as my thanks.

LORD V. Did Sir George pay the two hundred
and forty pounds, Mr. Thompfon?

THOM. The note, which he pretended to write
and fend by me, was a draft on his banker for three
hundred.

LORD V. Why he confirmed all my arguments
againft it; and added twice as many of his own.

DR. Sair Shorge vas alvay make agréable. Dat
vas his fay.

LADY V.

LADY V. I own, however, I am still more surprised at the unexampled generosity of Mr. Delaval.

SCENE IX. *Enter* WILLIAMS.

LADY V. Where is your master, Mr. Williams?

WILL. They are all coming, my lady.

LADY V. Who is coming?

WILL. Mr. Delaval, Lady Jane, Miss Delaval, and Sir George. There has been sad work! But it is all over, and they are now so happy! Here they are!

SCENE THE LAST. *Enter Mr.* DELAVAL *leading* LADY JANE, *and* SIR GEORGE *with* MARIA, *followed by* LUCY.

LORD V. Mr. Delaval, I have great obligations to you. Thompson has been telling me of your disinterested equity.

DEL. The obligation, my lord, was mine. Your lordship well knows that the first of obligations is to be just.

LORD V. Well, well; but the estate you are so willing to resign will still, I hope, be yours.

DEL. Nay, my lord.

LORD V. Dubious as all things are, that is a subject on which I protest I do not believe I shall ever have any doubts. What say you, Lady Jane? *(Irony)* But now I have my doubts again.

LADY J. *(Eagerly)* What doubts, my lord?

LORD V. I doubt whether you understand me?

LADY J. Would your lordship teach me to dissemble?

LORD V. Um—I doubt whether that would be much for your good.

DEL.

DEL. I hope Lady Vibrate will not oppose our union?

LADY V. No, Mr. Delaval. Your laſt generous action has charmed me; and Sir George—

SIR G. Has declined in your good opinion. But you cannot think ſo ill of me as I do of myſelf; and, if ever again I ſhould recover my own ſelf reſpect, I ſhall be indebted for it to this beſt of men, and to this moſt incomparable and affectionate of women!

MAR. My preſent joys are inexpreſſible!

DEL. Which my impetuous indignation threatened for ever to deſtroy. *(Comes forward)* How dangerous are extremes! Sometimes we doubt, and indeciſion is our bane: at others, hurried away by the ſudden impulſe of paſſion, our courſe is marked with miſery. One man is too compliant: another too intractable. Yet happineſs is the aim of all. Since then all are ſo liable to be miſled, let gentle forbearance, indulgent thoughts, and a mild forgiving ſpirit, be ever held as the ſacred duties of man to man.

[EXEUNT OMNES.

EPILOGUE.

SPOKEN BY MR. QUICK, AND MRS. MATTOCKS.

(As Mr Pope concludes and is preparing to bow to the audience,
Mr Quick with some importance comes forward.)

Mr. Q. HOLD, Mr. Pope! Pleafe to give place to me:

'Tis my part to conclude the comedy.

 Hem! Hem!   *(Begins a grave and ftately bow.)*

Mrs. M. *(Eagerly advancing.)* Yours, Mr. Quick? I beg you'll
   hold your tongue!

All Epilogues of right to me belong.

You teafe the audience, fir; and put me out.

Mr. Q. Teafe? Humph! Permit me, madam, there to doubt.

Mrs. M. Your part is over, now; your *doubts* are ended.

Mr. Q. Would that they were! *(To the audience.)* Say, friends,
   are you offended?

Or are you pleas'd? Which way do you incline?

The author has his doubts; and I have mine;

Pronounce our doom: relieve us from our pain!

Mrs. M. *(Laughs.)* Look at thofe difmal features and refrain.

Mr. Q. Should it be fatal, hear, oh hear, our pleadings!

Grant an arreft of judgment: ftay proceedings:

I move the court——

Mrs. M.   You move? Stand back! I'll wait no longer.

I tell you once again I am th' Epilogue monger.

   (Surveys him and laughs)

Mr. Q. What do you laugh at?

Mrs. M.   You! There's reafon ample!

Mr. Q. *(Retiring.)* I beg, firs, you'll not follow her example.

         Mrs. M.

Mrs. M. The hypocrite! Well, well, I'm glad he's gone:
For now the *pleadings* will be all my own.
The author hopes I'll advocate his play.
Heaven help the man! What would he have me say?

     (Recollecting.)

Something about the anxious months he spent,

     (Pompously)

His garret traversing his brain intent
On this, and that, and t'other; action, plot,
Wit, humour, passion; and the lord knows what!
And tell how difficult it was to write ·
The charming nonsense you have heard to-night! ——
Poor fool! When he suppos'd his work complete,
He thought he had achiev'd a mighty feat!
Nay he protests that earth and heaven he'd move,
Could he but pen what you might well approve.
The man speaks fair; is tolerably civil:
Then, since an author's only a poor devil,
Doom him to what will give us all delight:
Make him repeat his follies every night.

THE END.

www.ingramcontent.com/pod-product-compliance
Lightning Source LLC
Chambersburg PA
CBHW020027030726
47499CB00007B/2304